ORCHARD BOOKS

First published in Great Britain in 2017 by The Watts Publishing Group

1 3 5 7 9 10 8 6 4 2

HASBRO and its logo, MY LITTLE PONY and all related characters are trademarks of Hasbro and are used with permission.

© 2017 Hasbro. All rights reserved.

A CIP catalogue record for this book is

available from the British Library

ISBN 978 1 40835 064 5

Printed and bound in China

Orchard Books
An imprint of Hachette Children's Group
Part of The Watts Publishing Group Limited
Carmelite House
50 Victoria Embankment
London EC4Y 0DZ

An Hachette UK Company
www.hachette.co.uk

www.hachettechildrens.co.uk

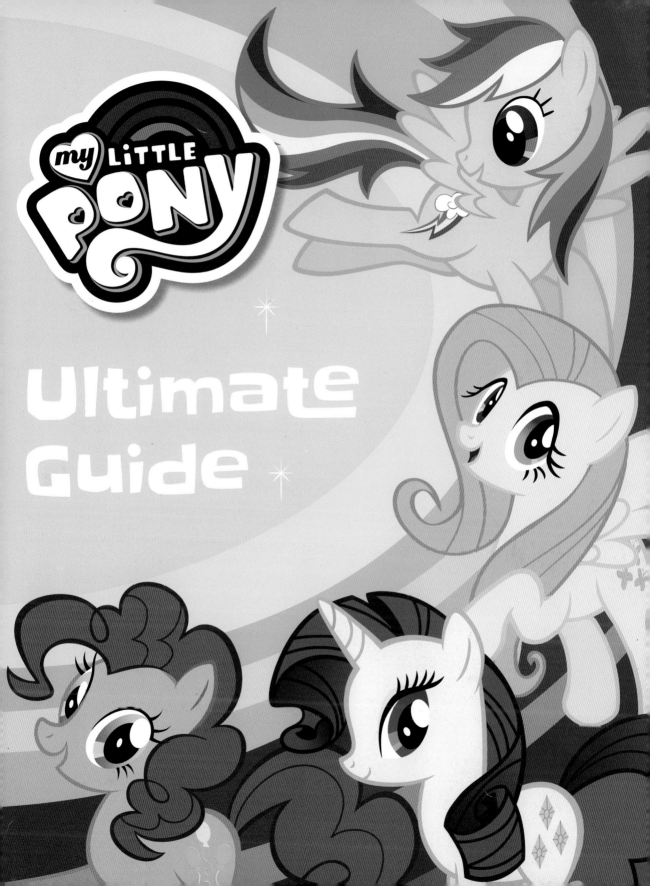

My Little Pony

Ultimate Guide

Contents

How It All Began!

Hello there, friends!

My name is Princess Twilight Sparkle and I am so pleased to you welcome to this very special book! Inside you'll find everything you need to know about me and my pony friends, a guide to all the wonderful places in Equestria, and all our most exciting adventures.

The incredible land of Equestria is ruled by Princess Celestia. She reigns over our magical kingdom with kindness and wisdom, alongside her sister, Princess Luna. Princess Celestia has been my mentor ever since I was young.

I love learning, and through my research and reading, I discovered that Equestria wasn't always such a peaceful, harmonious place. Before we begin our journey across Equestria, meeting the amazing ponies who live there, it's time to go back in time for a very special tale …

Once upon a time,

in the magical land of Equestria,

There were two regal sisters who ruled together
and created harmony for all the land.

To do this, the eldest, Celestia, used her
magic to raise the sun at dawn ...

while the younger, Luna, brought out
the moon to begin the night.

Thus, the two sisters maintained balance
for their kingdom and the ponies who lived there.

But as time went on, the younger sister became resentful. The ponies relished playing in the daytime that her elder sister brought forth ...

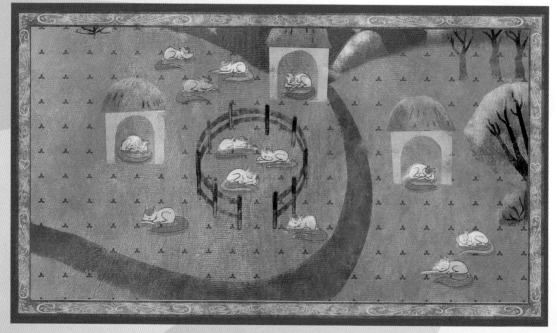

but shunned and slept through her beautiful night.

One fateful day, Luna refused to lower
the moon to make way for the dawn.

Celestia tried to reason with her younger sister.
But the bitterness in Luna's heart had transformed her
into a wicked mare of darkness ... Nightmare Moon!

Nightmare Moon vowed that she would
shroud the land in eternal night.

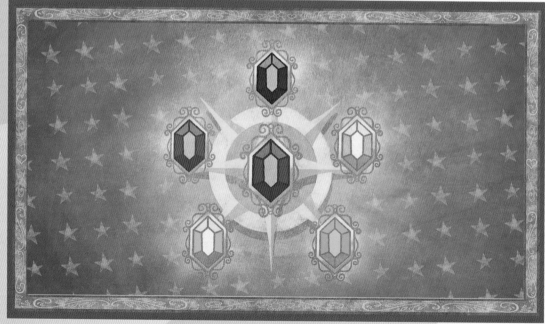

Reluctantly, Celestia harnessed the most powerful
magic known to Ponydom: the Elements of Harmony!

Using the magic of the Elements of Harmony, she defeated Nightmare Moon and banished her sister permanently into the moon. Princess Celestia took on responsibility for both the sun and the moon, and harmony has been maintained in Equestria ever since.

So for many hundreds of years, all had been well in Equestria, and everypony believed that the myth was just an old tale. But then I discovered a terrifying truth that would shatter the peace and harmony of our beloved home. On the longest day of the thousandth year – the day of the Summer Sun Celebration – Nightmare Moon would return and bring with her eternal night.

I tried to tell Princess Celestia but she insisted that I should focus on the upcoming Summer Sun Celebration, an annual event which was taking place in Ponyville on the longest day of the year ...

How Twilight Sparkle Came to Ponyville

As Princess Celestia's most faithful student, I was the only one she could trust to get things just right for the Summer Sun Celebration, being held in Ponyville that year. And so I travelled to Ponyville with Spike, my faithful dragon assistant.

Princess Celestia also hoped I'd make some friends in Ponyville. She worried that I spent too much time with my head in my books. At least our home in Ponyville would be the Golden Oak Library ... after all, you never know when you might want to do a little light reading!

But first it was time to make sure that everypony was well prepared for the Summer Sun Celebration, which was due to start the very next day.

Summer Sun Celebration Checklist

☐ Banquet – Applejack
☐ Clearing the Clouds – **Rainbow Dash**
☐ Decorations – Rarity
☐ Music – Fluttershy

Banquet - Applejack

The first pony to check up on was Applejack, who lived at Sweet Apple Acres. Within minutes she had introduced me to her whole family and I was stuffed full of the most delicious treats and bakes – all made from apples of course. Applejack surely was the most honest and welcoming pony I'd ever met!

Clearing the Clouds - Rainbow Dash

After knocking me into a muddy puddle and then soaking me with a raincloud, I wasn't sure how much I liked Rainbow Dash. This speedy Pegasus pony seemed more concerned with joining the Wonderbolts aerobatic team than making the weather perfect for the celebrations! But I soon realised she was very loyal and a lot of fun.

Decorations - Rarity

Spike was certainly impressed with Rarity – I've never seen him so bowled over by anypony! And this elegant Unicorn had won me over too. Not only did she have lots of great ideas for decorations but she was determined to make me look my best and was so generous with her time and advice.

Music - Fluttershy

It was clear right away that everyone loved Fluttershy – including all the creatures of Equestria. And it was easy to see why – this shy and gentle pony was full of kindness. Fluttershy had never seen a baby dragon before and she was very excited to meet Spike! Fluttershy was working with her bird friends to make magical music for the Summer Sun Celebration. I couldn't wait to hear it!

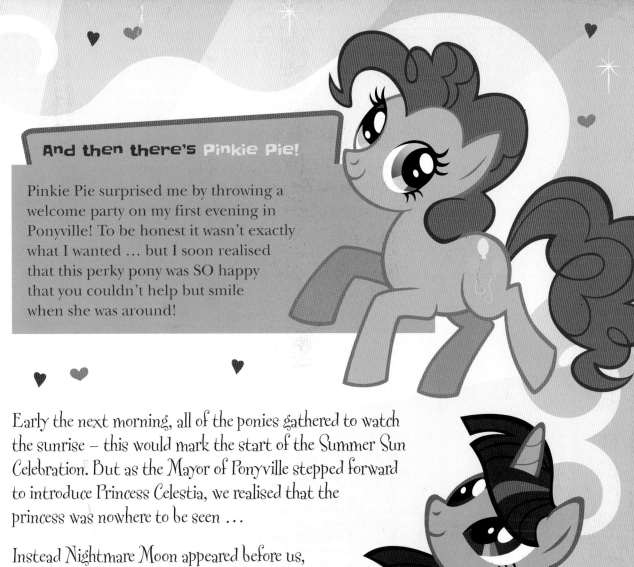

And then there's Pinkie Pie!

Pinkie Pie surprised me by throwing a welcome party on my first evening in Ponyville! To be honest it wasn't exactly what I wanted ... but I soon realised that this perky pony was SO happy that you couldn't help but smile when she was around!

Early the next morning, all of the ponies gathered to watch the sunrise – this would mark the start of the Summer Sun Celebration. But as the Mayor of Ponyville stepped forward to introduce Princess Celestia, we realised that the princess was nowhere to be seen ...

Instead Nightmare Moon appeared before us, threatening the whole of Equestria with eternal night. I knew I had to do something to save our beloved ruler – and I needed the help of five very special ponies.

So together we set off on our very first adventure, which would change all our lives and show me the true meaning of friendship. You'll find out what happened later in this book, but first, my pony friends are waiting to meet you ...

The Mane Six
(and Spike)

Applejack

Applejack is one of the kindest, most down-to-earth ponies in all of Equestria. She is NEVER afraid to get her hooves dirty working the land at Sweet Apple Acres. She is as honest as a pony comes and anypony can depend on her to help in a crisis.

Applejack lives at Sweet Apple Acres, where the orchards are overflowing with fresh fruit, including delicious Zap apples. Looking after the farm is hard work and Applejack and her (very large!) family have to pull together to get things done.

Applejack is one strong pony and one way she keeps up her strength is to eat … a LOT! It's a good job that there's never a shortage of pies, strudels, fritters and apple sauce down on the family farm. Delicious!

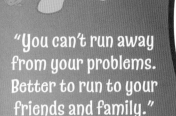

"You can't run away from your problems. Better to run to your friends and family."

"Thanks, y'all. I guess I just got so used to doin' everythin' a certain way, I didn't realise there were any problems."

Occupation:
Farmer

Type of pony:
Earth pony

Family:
Granny Smith, younger sister Apple Bloom, older brother Big McIntosh — plus a HUGE extended family!

Cutie mark:
Three apples

Element of Harmony
HONESTY

DID YOU KNOW?
Applejack once saved Ponyville from being stampeded to the ground by a herd of buffalo. She was awarded a trophy for her courage!

Best qualities:
Loyal, honest, kind, hard-working, strong

Worst qualities:
Stubborn, doesn't like to admit when things become too much for her!

Applejack's Best Bits!

VIP tree-tment ... Applejack makes sure her beloved apple tree, Bloomberg, gets his own bed on the train journey to Appleloosa, where she eventually plants him.

Applejack won't go anywhere without her Stetson hat – she even wears it to be a bridesmaid at Princess Cadance's wedding!

Applejack's ENORMOUS appetite is famous ...

Strong and true ... All her friends agree that Applejack is one amazing pony!

Rainbow Dash

Rainbow Dash is confident, competitive, fearless – and fast! A Pegasus pony, she zooms through the air and can clear clouds out of the sky with a mighty flip and a kick.

A loyal and true friend, Rainbow Dash will help her pony pals take on evil villains and fierce foes with bags of courage to spare. She achieved her lifetime goal of joining the high-flying aerobatic team the Wonderbolts, and now she shows off her impressive aerial skills with the best of the best!

Rainbow Dash lives in Ponyville but originally comes from Cloudsdale, an amazing cloud city in the sky. Only Pegasus ponies are able to walk on the clouds, so if Earth ponies or Unicorns want to visit, they need to ride on a hot-air balloon – or use a little magic!

"I could clear this sky in ten seconds flat!"

"Danger's my middle name. Rainbow 'Danger' Dash!"

"No matter what your sport is ... you gotta give it your best shot!"

Occupation:
Ponyville weather patrol, member of the Wonderbolts

Type of pony:
Pegasus pony

Family:
It's a mystery!

Cutie mark:
Cloud and lightning bolt

Element of Harmony
LOYALTY

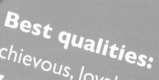

DID YOU KNOW?
Rainbow Dash's favourite flying moves include the "rainbow dry" and the "super-speed strut"!

Best qualities:
Mischievous, loyal, funny

Worst qualities:
Very competitive, can be over-confident

Rainbow Dash's Best Bits!

Rainbow Dash's home is the lofty Cloudominium, located high in the skies above Ponyville.

Rainbow Dash performs a Sonic Rainboom while diving to rescue Rarity, whose magical wings have failed.

Up in flames ... Rainbow flies into a storm cloud during her first disastrous aerial performance with the Wonderbolts!

Proud Pegasus! Rainbow Dash is crowned Best Young Flyer at the Cloudseum in Cloudsdale.

Stand-off! Rainbow Dash and Applejack can't resist a bit of healthy competition, including dares!

Flying high! Rainbow achieves her lifelong dream of becoming a Wonderbolt!

Night-time ninja! While in hospital, Rainbow discovers a love of reading, but decides to keep it secret from her friends. Here she is, on her way to find her book …

Hero hug! Rainbow Dash with her idol, the explorer Daring Do.

Rarity

Rarity is a pony of exquisite taste, especially when it comes to her friends! She can see just how fabulous everypony is on the inside. Rarity believes that a pony's outer beauty should reflect their inner beauty – so she is full of fashion ideas to make everypony shine!

Whether Rarity is choosing an elegant fabric for castle curtains or creating outfits for her three clothing boutiques, she makes sure ALL her designs are divine! She is generous with her compliments, yet she is always genuine.

Rarity has a stunning cat companion called Opalescence. With long white fur, a perfect purple bow and bejewelled collar, Opal is every bit as glamorous as her owner. But unlike generous Rarity, Opal can be a little snobby and rude. If Opal doesn't like you, you'll soon know it!

"Welcome to Carousel Boutique, where every garment is chic, unique and magnifique."

"You should never forget that you are the product of your home and your friends, and that is something to always be proud of, no matter what!"

Occupation:
Fashion designer, seamstress, boutique owner

Type of pony:
Unicorn

Family:
Parents Hondo Flanks and Cookie Crumbles, younger sister Sweetie Belle

Cutie mark:
Three diamonds

Element of Harmony
GENEROSITY

DID YOU KNOW?
Rarity HATES to get muddy or wet. This is one pony who always likes to look her best.

Best qualities:
Creative, hard-working, determined, kind

Worst qualities:
Can be overly dramatic, can get carried away with her ideas

Rarity's Best Bits!

Pegasus pretender ... Rarity gets carried away, showing off the magical wings that Twilight Sparkle has made for her!

This hard-working pony also does drama ... big time!

Rarity works hard at her success. She's always busy creating unique and beautiful designs for her friends and customers.

Rarity adores her little sis, Sweetie Belle ...

... she also adores her "spiritual home", Manehattan!

When Rainbow Dash is accused of a crime she didn't commit, loyal friend Rarity turns detective ...

Mirror, mirror on the wall ... This perfect pony can be a little vain sometimes!

Hooficure, anypony? The La-Ti-Da Spa is one of Rarity's favourite places in Ponyville.

Fluttershy

As a young Pegasus pony living in Cloudsdale, quiet Fluttershy didn't fit in with the other fast-flying Pegasi. But she soon learned she had a natural talent for caring for animals. Now she lives on the edge of the peaceful Everfree Forest, in a cottage full of creatures!

When Fluttershy first met Twilight Sparkle on the day before the Summer Sun Celebration, she was almost too shy to tell Twilight her name! However, as soon as Fluttershy saw Spike she relaxed and became much more chatty.

Fluttershy's special animal companion is a tiny white rabbit called Angel Bunny. Angel may look sweet and innocent with his big eyes and tiny pink nose, but he can be very demanding! He also looks after Fluttershy, reminding her to stand up for herself and not to forget important events or occasions.

"I was worried that I'd fail every time! Sometimes you have to do things, even though you might fail."

"If you just keep your head high, do your best, and believe in yourself, anything can happen!"

Occupation:
Animal carer, part-time Pony Tones singer

Type of pony:
Pegasus pony (but prefers to keep her hooves on the ground)

Family:
Parents Mr and Mrs Shy, brother Zephyr Breeze

Cutie mark:
Three butterflies

DID YOU KNOW?
Fluttershy has a special "Stare" she can use to make creatures behave the way she wants them to. Kind Fluttershy only employs this power when she really needs to.

Element of Harmony
KINDNESS

Best qualities:
Graceful, gentle, musical, patient

Worst qualities:
Very shy and prone to panic!

Fluttershy's Best Bits!

Fluttershy extends the hoof of friendship to troublemaker Discord.

Tuneful Fluttershy conducts the songbird choir at Cadance and Shining Armor's wedding.

Watch out, Equestria, it's ... the Stare!

Fluttershy loves ALL creatures, from tiny Breezies ...

... to giant three-headed dogs. Cerberus enjoys his tummy rub!

Timid Fluttershy has a beautiful singing voice – but it takes a lot of courage to overcome her stage fright and appear on stage with the Pony Tones.

Alter ego! When the ponies are sucked into the comic book world of the Power Ponies, Fluttershy becomes "Saddle Rager" – a huge muscular monster!

When a spell of Twilight Sparkle's backfires, gentle Fluttershy turns into a terrifying FLUTTERBAT!

Pinkie Pie

Pinkie Pie is energetic, zany, giggly and full of FUN! She loves any excuse for a party, be it a welcome party, a birthday party or a cutie mark party – her party cannon is always at the ready!

Pinkie may be full of beans but sometimes she lacks self-confidence. When a pony called Cheese Sandwich appeared one day and claimed to be the best party-planner in the whole of Equestria, Pinkie was crushed. She was determined to prove that she was the best, with disastrous results! But she realised that you can always learn from others … and that there's a place for everypony in Equestria.

Pinkie Pie works in Sugarcube Corner, Ponyville's bakery and sweet shop. It's the perfect place for this sweet-as-sugar pony! Living and working alongside Pinkie is her pet alligator, Gummy, who likes to nibble on cakes, biscuits … or even Pinkie Pie. It's a good job he doesn't have any teeth!

"I'd never felt joy like that before! It felt so good I just wanted to keep smiling for ever!"

"Oh, I never leave home without my party cannon."

"Parties. Are. Serious!"

Occupation:
Baker, caterer, awesome party organiser

Type of pony:
Earth pony

Family:
Parents Igneous Rock and Cloudy Quartz, and sisters Maud Pie, Limestone Pie and Marble Pie

Cutie mark:
Three balloons

DID YOU KNOW?

When Pinkie Pie is happy, her mane and tail get "poufy"! When she is sad or unhappy, they lie flat.

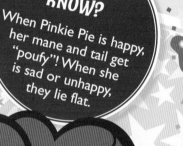

Element of Harmony
LAUGHTER

Best qualities:
Happy, welcoming, kind, has a brilliant memory

Worst quality:
Sometimes lacks self-confidence

Pinkie Pie's Best Bits!

Pinkie Pie uses her party cannon to help defeat the changelings and save Princess Celestia's wedding. That's Party Power!

Parties, and making everypony laugh, were always Pinkie's calling! Here she is juggling rubber chickens as a filly ...

Does anypony recognise Pinkie Pie? This perky pony loves a disguise!

Party rivals! Pinkie challenges party-planner Cheese Sandwich to a "goof-off" ...

... but she soon finds that the best parties happen when ponies work together!

When Pinkie Pie thinks her friends don't want to come to her parties any more, she invites Mr Turnip, Sir Linsalot and Madame le Flour.

Pinkie is SO good at ice skating she can do it standing on her head!

Too much of a good thing ... When Pinkie Pie clones herself by stepping into the mirror pool, the Pinkies cause havoc all over Ponyville!

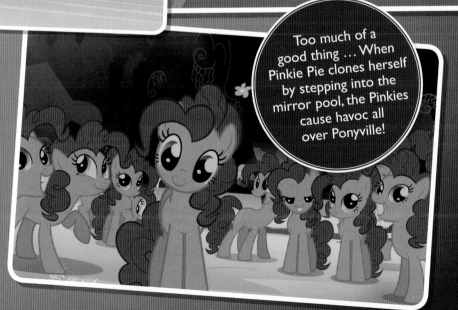

Twilight Sparkle

Nopony knows more about Equestria, magic and friendship than Princess Twilight Sparkle! But did you know that Twilight wasn't always a princess ...

Twilight was sent to Ponyville to oversee the annual Summer Sun Celebration and learn about friendship. Here she met her five best friends and together they discovered the magical Elements of Harmony (see p. 128).

(see p. 128)

This powerful magic – the magic of friendship – allows Twilight and her friends to protect Equestria from the villains who wish to harm it. There was a grand celebration in Canterlot when Twilight became an Alicorn. She was later made Princess of Friendship by her mentor Princess Celestia.

Nowadays Twilight lives in the Castle of Friendship with her best friend and assistant, Spike, and a helpful owl named Owlowiscious! She also has a student of her own, Starlight Glimmer.

"We've learned that friendship isn't always easy, but there's no doubt it's worth fighting for!"

"Reading is something everypony can enjoy, if they just give it a try."

Occupation:
Princess of Friendship, mentor to Starlight Glimmer

Type of pony:
Alicorn (formerly a Unicorn)

Family:
Parents Twilight Velvet and Night Light, brother Shining Armor

Cutie mark:
Pink sparkle

Element of Harmony
MAGIC

DID YOU KNOW?
Twilight is scared of quesadillas!

Best qualities:
Logical, patient, determined, well organised

Worst quality:
Gets stressed under pressure

41

Twilight Sparkle's Best Bits!

Even as a filly, Twilight loved books and studying. Her parents enrolled her in Princess Celestia's School for Gifted Unicorns in Canterlot.

It's not unusual for Twilight to fall asleep with a book in her hooves after a long night's studying ...

Never look a cockatrice in the eye! Twilight did – and was turned to stone. Luckily Fluttershy persuaded the scary bird-snake to return her friend to normal ...

Twilight excels at lots of things ... but not ice skating!

Pink power! Twilight's horn glows bright pink when she is using her powerful magic ...

Brilliantly bearded ... Twilight's favourite character to dress up as is her hero, the ancient sorcerer Star Swirl the Bearded.

Seriously stressed! Twilight felt the pressure when she couldn't think of a friendship lesson to write about to Princess Celestia.

Scary! Twilight comes face to face with her future self – if she doesn't start relaxing!

Twilight is super organised and loves a checklist. Her assistant Spike is less keen!

Spike

He may not be a pony, but Spike and his pony pals are inseparable. Spike has known Twilight Sparkle his whole life. She even used her magic to help him hatch from his egg. It was the start of a lifelong friendship!

Spike is loyal and dedicated and these two traits make him Twilight's "number-one assistant". And another amazing skill? He can send and receive letters using his green fiery dragon breath! He often reads Princess Celestia's notes to Twilight when they're on an important royal mission.

While Spike isn't the biggest dragon around, he is resourceful and determined. He cherishes his friendships with the ponies and will do anything for them – and for Equestria!

"Today I learned how important it is to be honest with your friends when they're doing something that you don't think is right. A true friend knows that you're speaking up because you care about them."

"Twilight can find a rulebook for everything!"

DID YOU KNOW?

Spike has a MASSIVE crush on Rarity. He would do anything for his glamorous Unicorn friend.

Occupation:
Twilight Sparkle's assistant

Type:
Baby dragon

Family:
A mystery!

Cutie mark:
None

Best qualities:
Kind, loyal, devoted and helpful

Worst quality:
Spike can be lazy ... he just loves to sleep (especially when it's raining outside)

Spike's Best Bits!

You don't want to catch a cold from this baby dragon. He sneezes green fire! Yuck!

In their comic book caper, Spike saves his friends, the Power Ponies, from the evil Mane-iac – proving that you shouldn't judge a dragon by his size!

Spiky buddies … Spike takes pity on Thorax the Changeling, and persuades the ponies of the Crystal Empire to accept him as a friend.

All creatures great and small … Spike earns the respect of the buffalo herd.

Amazing Equestria

Equestria is a land like no other. It has sparkling cities, icy mountains, deserts, forests and oceans – all kept safe and in balance by the power of friendship. Here is your special guide to the key places in this truly magical land ...

CANTERLOT
Capital city
Sophisticated
Home to the royal family

CRYSTAL EMPIRE
Majestic
Glittering
Full of heart

PONYVILLE
Friendly
Bustling
Cosy

EVERFREE FOREST
Home to many unusual creatures
Mysterious
Magical

MOUNT EVERHOOF
32,000 HOOVES

CRYSTAL EMPIRE

FROZEN NORTH

YAKYAKISTAN

NORTH LUNA OCEAN

YANHOOVER

GALLOPI GORG

UNICORN RAN

CANTERLOT

TWILIGHTS CASTLE

SADDLE L.

FAIL M

RAMBLIN

TALL TALE

SMOKEY MOUNTAINS

PONYVILLE

UNDISCOVERED WEST

WHITE TAIL WOODS

EVERFREE FOREST

BOGG

GHASTLY GORGE

LOS PEGASUS

APPLEWOOD

SAN PALOMINO DESERT

ROCK FARM

MACINTOSH HILLS

MYSTERIOUS SOUTH

SOUTH

LUNA OCEAN

ARIMASPI TERRITORY

FORBID

50

INTO THE UNKNOWN

YAKET RANGE

BUG
BEAR
TERRITORY

MANEHATTAN
Big city
Fashionable
Theatrical

MOUNTAINS

STARLIGHTS VILLAGE

MANEHATTAN

TROTTINGHAM

GRIFFONSTONE
STATION

GRIFFISH
ISLES

GUTO RIVER

HOLLOW
SHADES

FILLY
DELPHIA

YONDER
TO
GRIFFONS

GRIFFONSTONE

BALTIMARE

CELESTIAL
SEA

The Founding of Equestria

Many years ago the three main tribes of ponies – Earth ponies, Unicorns and Pegasi – lived apart and only cared for their own kind. But one day a terrible blizzard arrived and caused the ponies to struggle and starve. After many moons of suffering, the leaders of the three tribes realised that the blizzard was caused by windigos – winter spirits that feed off hatred and war. The only way for the tribes to defeat these creatures was to make peace and work together.

For the sake of their starving ponyfolk, the three leaders decided to join forces and live in a kingdom shared peacefully by all three tribes. They named their new land Equestria – and peace and happiness reigned!

Welcome to Ponyville!

Ponyville

Ponyville is the perfect place to meet new ponies. It's home to some of the sweetest, most loyal and most creative ponies in all of Equestria.

The History of Ponyville

Once Ponyville was nothing more than fields. Princess Celestia gave the Apple Family some land near the Everfree Forest, and this is where Granny Smith and her family planted their first orchard.

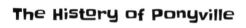

As a young filly, Granny Smith ventured into the Everfree Forest one night to look for food. She discovered trees that bore rainbow-coloured apples. She returned home with a bag full of them, and the next day she and her father planted the first Zap apple seeds.

Hearing about the delicious jam made from the Zap apples, other ponies started coming to the area. They built cosy homes with timber frames and thatched roofs, and many of them set up shops and businesses. Before they knew it, a friendly little town had established itself.

DID YOU KNOW?

Each year the ponies of Ponyville take part in a town tradition called the "Winter Wrap-Up" – an annual clean-up that prepares the land for spring.

Ponyville is home to Earth ponies, Unicorns and Pegasi, living in harmony.

Busy and Bustling!

Today Ponyville has everything a modern pony needs, including a train station, school, hospital, library, town hall, shops and restaurants! The ponies who live here also love to enjoy themselves, so there's a theatre and a spa for a bit of much-needed down-time!

A Tour of Ponyville

Marketplace

The marketplace is where everypony comes to do their shopping. The stalls and shops sell everything from fruit and vegetables to books and party supplies. Applejack and her family always have a cart at the market selling their delicious apples and apple products.

Schoolhouse

All young ponies go to school to learn reading, writing and pony PE. Cheerilee is the teacher at the Ponyville Schoolhouse. This kind filly is very knowledgeable and her young pupils adore her.

Healing Hospital

Ponyville hospital is housed in a grand old building with its own large gardens. Pound Cake and Pumpkin Cake – the baby foals of Mr and Mrs Cake – were born in the hospital and looked after by kind Nurse Redheart. Rainbow Dash has ended up at Ponyville Hospital several times after flying mishaps!

Train Station

You can take a train from Ponyville to almost anywhere in Equestria! If you travel to the Crystal Empire by train, you get the most beautiful views of the sparkling city as you approach. Two train conductors make sure that all ponies buy tickets for their journeys and don't miss their stops!

La-Ti-Da Spa

In need of a little relaxation after your busy tour of Ponyville? Look no further than the day spa! Rarity and Fluttershy often meet here for some pony pampering. And Spike is a big fan too!

Town Hall

The town hall is at the centre of Ponyville's town square. This is where the citizens of Ponyville meet on important occasions, such as to witness Princess Celestia raising the sun at the Summer Sun Celebration. Mayor Mare often gives speeches in the town hall or in the square outside!

Shops Galore

If you can't pick up what you need at the market, there are plenty of other shops to visit! At Sugarcube Corner, you'll receive a warm welcome from Pinkie Pie (selling some "interesting" flavours of cupcake!). Rainbow Dash's favourite store is the joke shop – it has all you need to play pranks on your pals! And to keep up to date with the latest fashions, be sure to pay a visit to Rarity's Carousel Boutique!

Theatre

This is the place to go to watch pony performances and plays. Sweetie Belle LOVES to write plays but even she has to admit that not all of them are good enough to make it on to the stage!

The Apple Family

Sweet Apple Acres on the outskirts of Ponyville is home to the Apple family. This large clan has at least thirty family members, all of them hard-working Earth ponies. Granny Smith, Big McIntosh and Apple Bloom live with Applejack at Sweet Apple Acres, while other family members run apple farms all over Equestria.

Big McIntosh

Big Mac (as he's known to his friends) doesn't say a lot – his favourite responses are "Eeeyup" or "Nnope". Along with his sister, Applejack, this strong, loyal pony takes care of the heavy-duty farm work at Sweet Apple Acres. Big Mac has a fabulous, deep singing voice and is a member of the popular Pony Tones singing group.

Granny Smith

This elderly filly may be getting on in years but she can still make the BEST apple pie in town! Granny Smith was one of the founding ponies of Ponyville, helping to set up the town by planting the first orchard. She is liked and respected by everypony.

Apple Bloom

This young filly is very close to her big sister Applejack and loves to learn from her ... although she sometimes thinks she can do things better than her big sis, leading to sisterly squabbles. But the two gals always make it up ... eventually!

Apple Bloom is one of the Cutie Mark Crusaders (or CMCs), and gets up to all kinds of adventures – and scrapes – with her best friends Sweetie Belle and Scootaloo.

Home Sweet Home

Earth ponies are known for their connection to the land, and the Apple family have this in bucket loads! The whole family are amazing farmers.

As well as a large apple orchard, Sweet Apple Acres produces corn and carrots. Yum!

DID YOU KNOW?

Pinkie Pie once found some evidence showing that she might be a distant cousin of Applejack's!

Some of the lesser-known Apple Family members include Apple Fritter, Apple Bumpkin, Red Gala, Red Delicious, Golden Delicious, Caramel Apple, Apple Strudel, Apple Tart, Half Baked Apple, Apple Brioche, Apple Cinnamon Crisp, Apple Cider, Apple Cobbler, Apple Honey, Apple Munchies, Gala Appleby, Lavender Fritter and Perfect Pie ... Phew!

Family Reunion

Once every 100 moons, the whole Apple Family gets together for races, apple snacks, hay rides and a barn dance. A family photograph is always taken on these special occasions. Smile, everypony!

The Cake Family

Best Bakers in Town?

Mr and Mrs Cake have some competition in the shape of Applejack and her family, who are well known for their apple-flavoured delicacies. (And, don't tell the Cakes we told you this, but Pinkie Pie once told Applejack that SHE was the best baker in town. Ssshh!)

Mr and Mrs Cake

Mr Carrot Cake and Mrs Cupcake are the owners of Sugarcube Corner, and two of the friendliest Earth ponies you'll ever meet. Mr and Mrs Cake love to bake. As well as running their shop, they cater for events and celebrations all over Ponyville, and their specialities include cake pops, cupcakes, rainbow cakes and cake-flavoured ice cream, packed with cake crumbs. Delicious!

Pumpkin Cake and Pound Cake

These adorable twins are the cutest little foals in Ponyville … but they are also small bundles of mischief! Pound Cake is a boy Pegasus and Pumpkin Cake is a girl Unicorn. It's very unusual to have twins belonging to a different tribe of pony, but as Mr Cake explains: "My great-great-great-great-grandfather was a Unicorn, and Cupcake's great-aunt's second cousin twice removed was a Pegasus!"

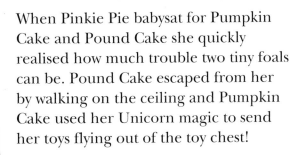

Double Trouble!

When Pinkie Pie babysat for Pumpkin Cake and Pound Cake she quickly realised how much trouble two tiny foals can be. Pound Cake escaped from her by walking on the ceiling and Pumpkin Cake used her Unicorn magic to send her toys flying out of the toy chest!

Home Sweet Home

Mr and Mrs Cake are very fond of Pinkie Pie and happily put up with all her zany behaviour, including her habit of setting off her party cannon in the shop! Pinkie lives above the shop and has worked for the Cakes ever since she moved to Ponyville.

The Cutie Mark Crusaders

The Cutie Mark Crusaders

The Cutie Mark Crusaders (or "CMCs" for short) is a club made up of Apple Bloom, Scootaloo and Sweetie Belle. The three friends were fed up of being called "blank flanks", the mean name given to ponies who have not yet got their cutie marks, so they decided to form their own club. The Crusaders' aim is to "work together to find out who we are and what we're supposed to be".

The three friends have tried out many different activities and missions in the hope of receiving their cutie marks – from mountain-climbing to mind-reading, hairdressing to chicken-herding, tightrope-walking to tiger-taming. Even when they finally did receive their marks (see p. 76), the Cutie Mark Crusaders stuck together and remained the best of friends!

Apple Bloom

Occupation: Cutie Mark Crusader and student

Type: Earth pony

Family: Little sister of Applejack and Big Mac, and granddaughter of Granny Smith

Cutie mark: A pink apple on a regal crest

Best qualities: Brave, loyal, kind

Worst qualities: Like her big sister, Apple Bloom can be stubborn. She is also rather clumsy … Oops!

"Maybe we'll get our cutie marks in stupidest ideas of all time." – Apple Bloom

"I'm in crystal heaven!"
– Sweetie Belle

Sweetie Belle

Occupation: Cutie Mark Crusader and student

Type: Unicorn

Family: Little sister of Rarity

Cutie mark: A pink star on a regal crest

Best qualities: Kind-hearted, positive, creative

Worst qualities: Can be vain at times and a bit of a dreamer

Hidden Headquarters

Applejack passed on her old clubhouse for the Crusaders to use as their headquarters. The Crusaders' closest friends always know where to find them – but no one else does!

DID YOU KNOW?
Each of the three CMCs represents a different tribe. Apple Bloom is an Earth pony, Scootaloo is a Pegasus and Sweetie Belle is a Unicorn.

DID YOU KNOW?
Speedy Scootaloo loves to whizz around Ponyville on her scooter … and creative Sweetie Belle has a lovely singing voice!

"I said, you got a problem with blank flanks?"
– Scootaloo

Scootaloo

Occupation: Cutie Mark Crusader and student

Type: Pegasus pony

Family: A mystery … although Scootaloo WISHES she were related to her hero Rainbow Dash!

Cutie mark: A pink lightning bolt on a regal crest

Best qualities: Energetic, friendly, fun

Worst qualities: Can be a bit defensive, often gets into arguments with Apple Bloom

Cutie Mark Pals

Diamond Tiara

Diamond Tiara grew up believing she was extra special just because she was wealthy. Her parents, Filthy Rich and Spoiled Rich, always told her that money was more important than friends – and so Diamond teased the other ponies and bossed them around.

All that changed when Diamond Tiara became friends with the Cutie Mark Crusaders. She finally stood up to her snooty mother and learned that her cutie mark wasn't about making demands and giving orders. Instead she found she could use her leadership talents in positive, unselfish ways. Behold a shiny new Diamond!

"This is my party! Everypony is supposed to be paying attention to me!" – Diamond Tiara

Silver Spoon

As Diamond Tiara's best friend, Silver Spoon never really stood up for herself – or anyone else. She giggled and sniggered when Diamond Tiara was horrid to others. But Silver has shown herself to be a loyal friend to Diamond Tiara, so hopefully in time she'll learn to be nice and supportive to everypony else …

Gabby the Griffon

Gabby the Griffon had always delivered the post in Griffonstone but she couldn't help feeling that she belonged elsewhere. So when she heard about cutie marks she was determined to travel to Ponyville and get one of her own.

The Cutie Mark Crusaders recognised Gabby as a "kindred spirit" – adventurous, gentle and kind. They carved a wooden cutie mark for Gabby and welcomed her as the first griffon member of the CMCs. Gabby vowed to take Cutie Mark Crusader values with her back to Griffonstone!

DID YOU KNOW?
Gabby is from Griffonstone, a city east of Equestria where only griffons live. Most griffons are rude and messy ... but not Gabby.

DID YOU KNOW?
Babs Seed started a Manehattan branch of the Cutie Mark Crusaders!

Babs Seed

This pony is Apple Bloom's cousin. She lives in Manehattan, but it was on a visit to Ponyville that she met her best friends, the Cutie Mark Crusaders. When Babs first arrived in Ponyville, she was mean to Apple Bloom and her friends, even taking over their clubhouse with Diamond Tiara and Silver Spoon. But after the Cutie Mark Crusaders showed her kindness, she stood up to Diamond and Silver Spoon and revealed her true self!

"We all have Cutie Marks now, and I'm always a friend to ponies who are still looking for theirs." – Babs Seed

School Days

Miss Cheerilee

This clever pony has lots of knowledge to pass on – from stories about the importance of cutie marks to the best ways of dealing with Discord. Miss Cheerilee likes to take her pupils out and about on trips, including tours of the Canterlot statue gardens and visits to the Manehattan museums. She always leads her class with kindness and understanding.

Pipsqueak

This little colt is big on personality! Fresh from Trottingham, he has a fabulous accent and a very thick forelock. While he may be smaller than other ponies, he has BIG ideas, like running successfully for student pony president.

Featherweight

A friend of the Cutie Mark Crusaders, Featherweight used to be the photographer for the *Foal Free Press*. But Miss Cheerilee decided he would make a great editor-in-chief – the job that had previously belonged to Diamond Tiara!

Snips and Snails

These two friends don't look much alike. Snips is short and squat, while Snails is long and lanky. But both of these laidback colts are total goofballs! They often sit at the back of the classroom, making jokes, playing pranks and getting into lots of mischief.

DID YOU KNOW?

Snips is the smallest pony in Ponyville!

Twist

At one time, Apple Bloom thought that Twist was the only other filly her age who didn't have a cutie mark. But just before Diamond Tiara's big party, Twist finally earned her mark: two candy canes in the shape of a heart. Perfect for the young, creative candy-maker.

Starlight Glimmer

Starlight Glimmer was the leader of a village where everypony had the same cutie mark. Twilight and her friends proved Starlight was a fraud, stealing the village ponies' cutie marks to make her own magic stronger!

DID YOU KNOW?

Starlight Glimmer is very skilled in using magic. Some say she could be as powerful as Twilight Sparkle!

When Starlight Glimmer used her magic to go back in time to destroy the bond of the six friends, Twilight and Spike were sucked back in time too! There, in the past, they learned how important the friendship of their other pony friends was to peace in Equestria. Twilight persuaded Starlight Glimmer to reverse her spell – but could she make Starlight understand the power of friendship? That's when Twilight decided to take on Starlight Glimmer as a student of magic and friendship. Starlight now lives with Twilight in the Castle of Friendship.

"I know what it's like to lead by fear and intimidation. And I know what it's like to want everypony to do what you say. But I was wrong. A real leader doesn't force her subjects to deny who they are. She celebrates what makes them unique and listens when one of them finds a better way!"

Occupation:
Previously the leader of "the town with no name" ... now Twilight's friend and student

Type of pony:
Unicorn

Family:
A mystery!

Cutie mark:
A star below a burst of magic

DID YOU KNOW?

Although Starlight has powerful magic, it has taken her a long time to grasp the magic of friendship. Luckily Twilight Sparkle has lots of patience with her pupil.

Best qualities:
Clever, charming, has a soft and shy side

Worst qualities:
Impatience, won't always devote enough time to her lessons

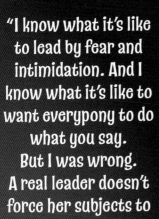

More Ponyville Ponies

Mayor Mare

Bulk Biceps

Cranky Doodle Donkey

Matilda

DID YOU KNOW?
Filthy Rich's grandfather Stinkin' Rich was one of the founders of Ponyville.

Filthy Rich

Spoiled Rich

Dr Horse

Nurse Redheart

Dr HoOves

Lemon Hearts

Twinkle Shine

Muffins

More Ponyville Ponies

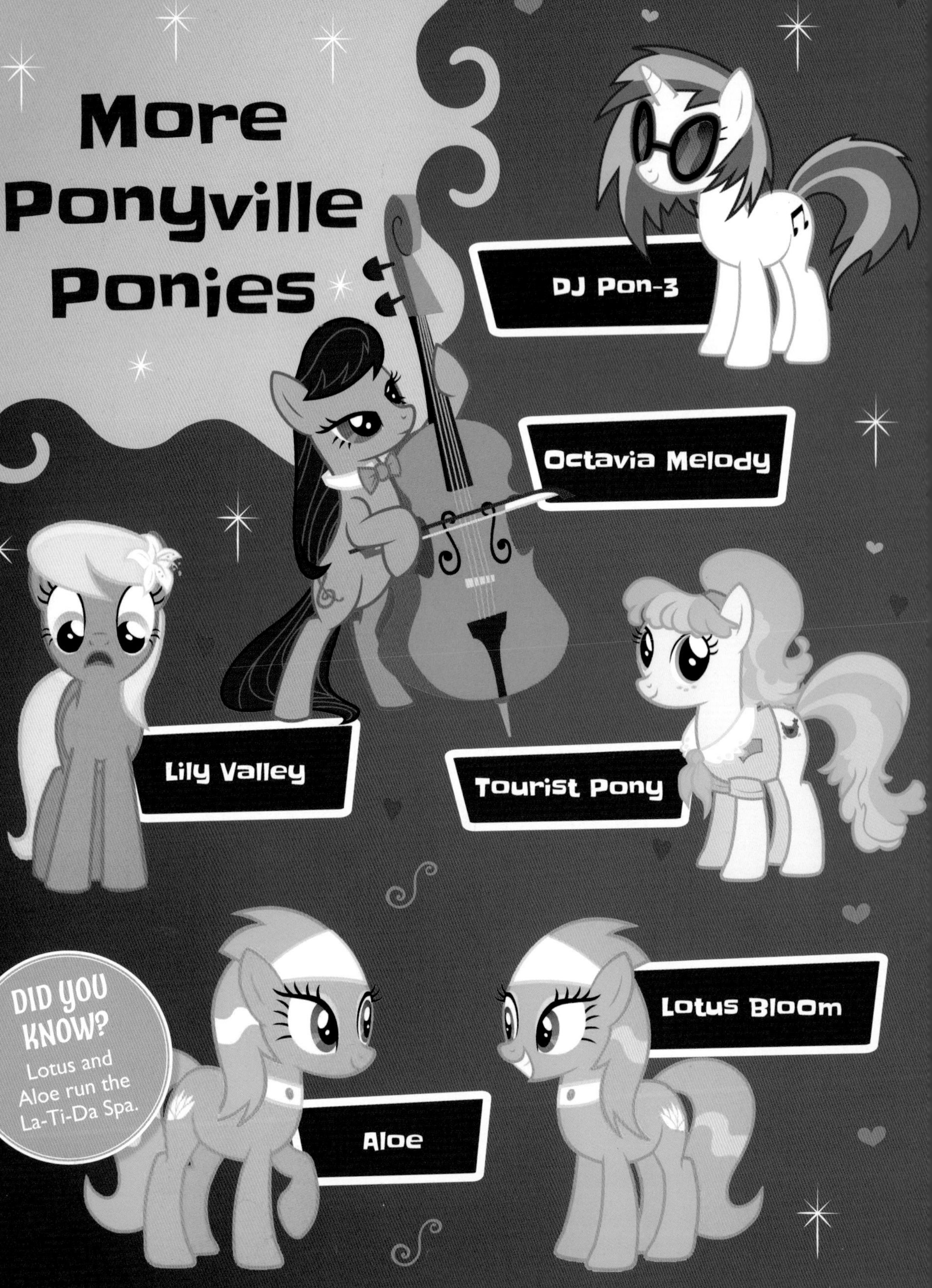

DJ Pon-3

Octavia Melody

Lily Valley

Tourist Pony

Lotus Bloom

Aloe

Daisy

Blossomforth

Golden Harvest

Rose

Lyra Heartstrings

Sweetie Drops

DID YOU KNOW?
Sweetie Drops is a secret agent, who works to keep Equestria safe!

73

Minuette

Market Sales Pony

Bowler Ponies

Strike

Cutie Mark Crusaders' Guide to **Cutie Marks!**

Magical Marks: The CMCs' Tale

Hi there, pony buds. It's Apple Bloom, Scootaloo and Sweetie Belle here – otherwise known as the CUTIE MARK CRUSADERS! For a long time, we tried EVERYTHING we could to make our cutie marks appear, but nothing seemed to work – until one day …

Our Story ...

Our classmate Pipsqueak decided to run for class president and he asked us, the CMCs, to be his campaign managers. We were happy to help as we knew he'd be a fair president and do his best for the school.

Pipsqueak was running against Diamond Tiara … and this spoilt pony wasn't going to give in without a fight. As Pip's campaign managers, we told everypony that it was time for a change. Vote Pipsqueak!

When Pip won the campaign, Diamond Tiara was very upset – and to make things worse, her mother was furious that she hadn't won. We felt so sorry for Diamond Tiara, especially when she revealed she wanted to be a better pony.

We decided that Diamond Tiara needed a friend – or three – to help her figure out how to change for the better. Back at our clubhouse, Diamond Tiara told us something surprising: she thought we were lucky NOT to have our cutie marks! How could that be?!

Diamond explained that her cutie mark had not helped her be a good pony. But we told her that she DID have it in her to change – and she listened. She stood up to her snooty mother and told her to stop being so mean!

Once Diamond Tiara realised that she could used her talents for good, she got straight to work, helping Pipsqueak fulfil all his campaign promises. We were so proud of her!

We realised that we had learnt a lesson too. It was FUN spending time helping other ponies, rather than just worrying about when our cutie marks would appear. And then something amazing happened …

… WE GOT OUR CUTIE MARKS! From then on, we knew our true destiny … to help other ponies discover theirs. We couldn't wait for the next adventure to begin!

Cutie Marks Explained

Want to know more about these marvellous marks? Here is our special guide to cutie marks and true destinies ...

Cutie Mark, Not a Beauty Mark

Every grown-up pony in Equestria has a cutie mark, and each one is as unique and special as the pony it belongs to. A cutie mark is linked to the pony's personality, skills or talent. Miss Cheerliee explains why three smiling flowers appeared as her cutie mark:

"The flowers symbolised my hope that I could help my future students bloom if I nurtured them with knowledge. The smiles represented the cheer I hoped to bring to my little ponies while they were learning!"

Patience, Everypony

It doesn't matter how much a young pony wants their cutie mark to appear – it will only happen when the time is right. Apple Bloom was desperate to get her cutie mark, even though big sister Applejack assured her that it would happen ... eventually!

DID YOU KNOW?

When a young pony gets his or her cutie mark, they celebrate by having a "cute-ceañera" party!

Messy Mix-up

Once Twilight Sparkle accidentally cast a spell that caused her friends' cutie marks to swap around, mixing up their destinies. Rarity tried to organise Ponyville's weather, Rainbow Dash attempted to look after Fluttershy's animal friends and Pinkie Pie took charge of Sweet Apple Acres. What a mess! Thankfully Twilight gave everypony back their own cutie mark in the end.

The Cutie Pox!

When Apple Bloom got the cutie pox, she gained more cutie marks than she could handle … As strange marks appeared, Apple Bloom had to use each skill they showed. She quickly wished she had NO cutie marks again! Luckily Zecora had a cure: a magical flower grown from the Seeds of Truth. Phew!

79

The Mane Six

A cutie mark is a reflection of a pony's special talent. We decided to ask our sisters and mentors how they received theirs ...

Twilight Sparkle's Story

Twilight Sparkle was trying out for a place at Princess Celestia's School for Gifted Unicorns. She had to make a dragon's egg hatch using magic. Nothing was working until a mysterious rainbow appeared in the sky and it kick-started Twilight's magic. The dragon egg hatched and Twilight's cutie mark appeared.

Pinkie Pie's Story

Pinkie Pie was working on her family's rock farm when an amazing rainbow appeared in the sky. It made Pinkie feel SO happy that she wanted to spread the feeling, so she threw a party for her family. As soon as she realised her destiny was to bring fun and joy into everypony's lives, her balloon cutie marks appeared.

DID YOU KNOW?

The baby dragon that hatched was SPIKE!

Fluttershy's Story

One day Fluttershy fell from her former home in Cloudsdale all the way down to the Everfree Forest. When a rainbow explosion scared the forest animals, Fluttershy was able to communicate with them and give them reassurance. Fluttershy's cutie mark appeared and her caring destiny was decided.

Rarity's Story

Rarity was struggling to find inspiration for her designs when her Unicorn horn led her to a mysterious rock. As a powerful rainbow explosion filled the sky, the rock cracked and glittering gems were revealed. The gems gave Rarity the inspiration she needed to create some truly sensational outfits. Her diamond cutie mark appeared that evening.

A BFF Bond

It's no coincidence that each pony's cutie mark arrived around the time that they spotted a mysterious rainbow. In fact, Rainbow Dash's Sonic Rainboom was the link between ALL of the pony friends. As Rarity says, "We've been BFFs for ever and we didn't even know it!"

Applejack's Story

When Applejack was a young filly, she decided to seek her destiny in the big city – Manehattan. But being a city pony was hard work and Applejack missed her home and her family. One morning a rainbow appeared and seemed to point the way home. Applejack realised where her destiny truly lay and as soon as she was back with her family at the ranch, her cutie mark appeared.

Rainbow Dash's Story

We all know how fast Rainbow Dash likes to fly … but on the day she got her cutie mark, this flying filly flew so fast that she created a Sonic Rainboom. No one had seen a Sonic Rainboom in Equestria for many hundreds of years. Rainbow's cutie mark appeared almost as quickly.

Cutie Mark Crusaders' Best Bits!

A fixer-upper ... On first sight, the CMCs are a little underwhelmed by their crumbling clubhouse.

Cutie YAY ... Those Crusaders really can make themselves heard!

Vast visitor ... Bulk Biceps is WAY too big for the Cutie Mark Crusaders' clubhouse!

82

Friends in free fall ... There are no limits to what the CMCs have done to earn their cutie marks!

Tightrope walking is just one of the many skills Apple Bloom discovered while she had the cutie pox.

Scootaloo gets a pep talk from her hero, Rainbow Dash, ahead of the Applewood Derby.

A job well done ... The CMCs find the perfect match for their teacher, Miss Cheerilee.

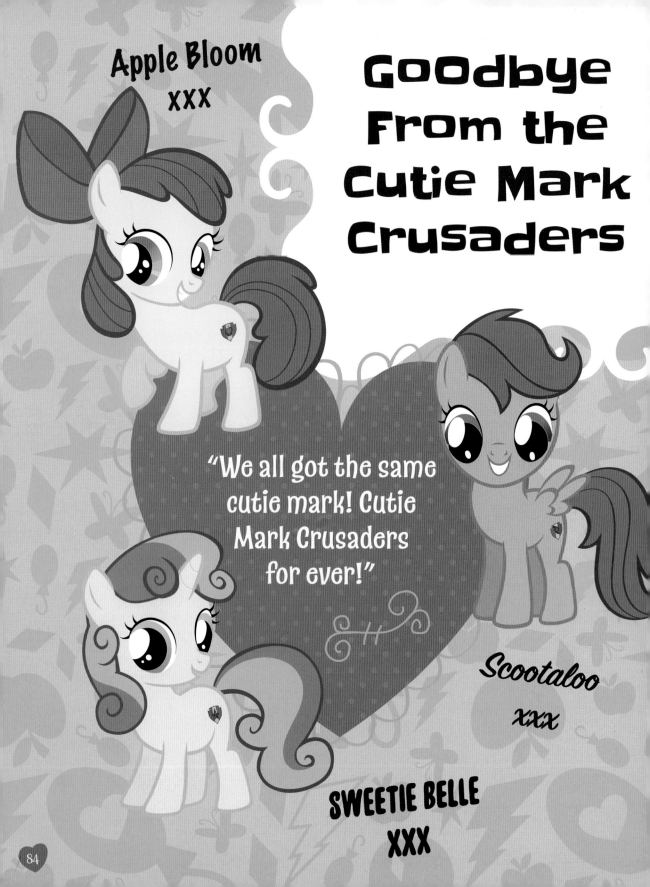

Canterlot

Perched on a steep mountainside in the very centre of the kingdom, Canterlot is the capital of Equestria. With its towering turrets and golden spires, it really is the most elegant city in the land. Princess Celestia and Princess Luna are its royal residents.

Glamorous Galas and Posh Parties

Canterlot hosts many of Equestria's most exclusive events – including the Grand Galloping Gala and the Canterlot Garden Party. The lucky ponies who attend are sure to wear their most fabulous clothes and accessories!

Canterlot Castle

Home to princesses Celestia and Luna, Canterlot Castle is a labyrinth of twisting corridors, elegant guest suites, stables and, of course, the Grand Hall. Prince Shining Armor and Princess Cadance's wedding was held here, as was Twilight Sparkle's coronation.

Talented Tots

The School for Gifted Unicorns is run by none other than Princess Celestia. Every Unicorn possesses magic and Princess Celestia encourages each of her students to nurture and develop their own unique skills and talents. Celestia's best known pupil is Twilight Sparkle, who looks up to her wise mentor in every way!

DID YOU KNOW?

Many years ago, precious gems were found below Canterlot. Beneath the castle are deep mines and many miles of winding tunnels.

DID YOU KNOW?

There's a train station in Canterlot, but the best way to arrive is by a flying chariot pulled by Pegasus ponies. This is how the princesses travel on special occasions!

Shop Till You Drop!

Canterlot has some of the best boutiques and shops in the land. Ponies will travel for miles to spend the day shopping and sipping tea at the chic cafés and restaurants. Rarity's Canterlot Carousel has been a huge hit, selling the finest couture to the city's best-dressed ponies!

All Hail, Princess Celestia!

Princess Perfection

You might say that Princess Celestia is wise beyond her years ... but in fact this kind and fair ruler is hundreds of years old! Her long flowing mane and tail are a rainbow of pastel colours that gleam against her sleek coat and graceful wings. Princess Celestia's wisdom and powerful magic help her maintain peace across Equestria – and her kindness and concern for the well-being of all of her subjects make her a beloved leader.

Royal Responsibilities

One of Celestia's greatest abilities is knowing how to share the responsibility of ruling Equestria. She puts great trust in the other members of the royal court. Her younger sister, Princess Luna, raises the moon each evening and takes charge during the nighttime.

Princess Cadance watches over the Crystal Empire, the enchanted realm that lies at the northern tip of Equestria. Cadance's husband, Shining Armor, shares this important job with her.

"Learning to trust your instincts is a valuable lesson to learn."

"I, Princess Celestia, hereby decree that the Unicorn Twilight Sparkle shall take on a new mission for Equestria. She must continue to study the magic of friendship. She must report to me her findings from her new home in Ponyville."

DID YOU KNOW?

Celestia's name comes from the word "celestial", which means "sky" or "heaven".

Occupation: Co-ruler of Equestria, princess, teacher, guardian of the day

Type of pony: Alicorn

Family: Older sister of Princess Luna and adoptive aunt of Princess Cadance

Cutie mark: The sun

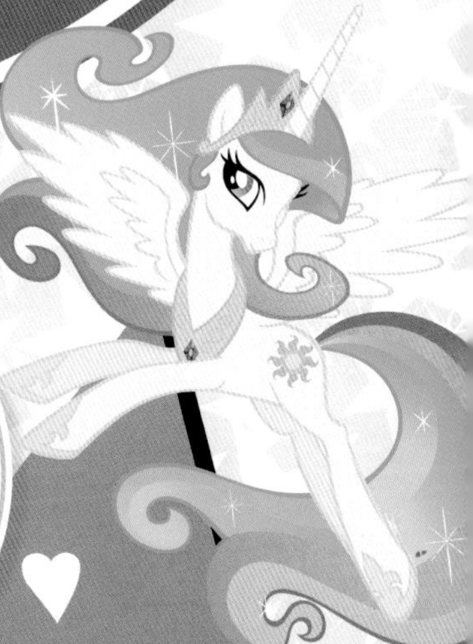

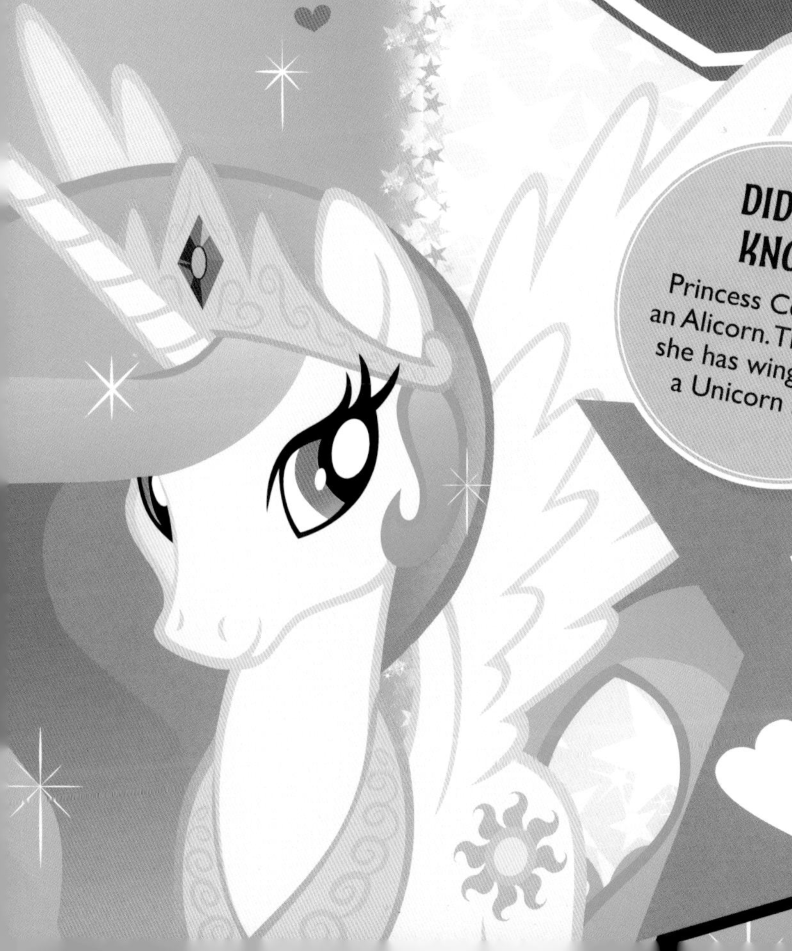

DID YOU KNOW?

Princess Celestia is an Alicorn. This means she has wings AND a Unicorn horn.

Best qualities: Kind, wise, forgiving, playful

Worst quality: Absolutely none!

All Rise For Princess Luna!

Starry Sister

Princess Luna shares responsibility for ruling Equestria with Princess Celestia, her older sister. When the afternoon grows long, it is Luna who raises the moon so night can come and the ponies can rest. With her indigo coat, purple mane and crescent-moon cutie mark, she has the perfect look for the guardian of the night.

No More Nightmares!

Ever since Nightmare Moon was defeated by the power of the Elements of Harmony, Princess Luna has been reunited with her caring older sister. Now she is striving to prove that she will only use her powers for good.

Playful Pony

When Princess Luna first returned to Equestria after being imprisoned in the moon, she spoke in a loud, harsh voice that scared the youngest ponies. It wasn't until Twilight Sparkle helped her on Nightmare Night that Luna learned to relax and have fun again.

"I am the princess of the night; thus it is my duty to come into your dreams."

"I understand what you're going through, Sweetie Belle. I too have a sister who often shines more brightly than me, and with this I have struggled."

Occupation: Co-ruler of Equestria, princess, guardian of the night

Type of pony: Alicorn

Family: Younger sister of Princess Celestia, aunt of Princess Cadance

Cutie mark: The moon

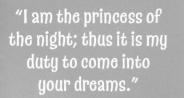

DID YOU KNOW?
The name Luna means "moon".

Best qualities:
A great listener, kind, fun, wants to do her best

Worst quality:
Can be jealous of her big sister … but tries her best not to let this take over!

DID YOU KNOW?
Princess Luna is in charge of the mystical realm of sleep and dreams. Only Luna can enter the dreams of other ponies.

The Crystal Couple: Cadance & Shining Armor

Romantic Rulers

Originally from Canterlot, Princess Cadance and Prince Shining Armor are the perfect couple – wise, strong, kind and fair. It was always their destiny to fall in love and rule the Crystal Empire side by side.

Super Sister-in-Law

When Twilight Sparkle found out that her brother was marrying Cadance, she was delighted. She knew Cadance was lots of fun, and kind and caring – after all, Cadance was Twilight's foal-sitter for many years when she was a young filly! Twilight loves her sister-in-law almost as much as she loves her big brother.

Princess Cadance

Occupation: Co-ruler of the Crystal Empire, princess (and former foal-sitter!)

Type: Alicorn

Family: Celestia's adopted niece

Cutie mark: A crystal heart

Best qualities: Fun, responsible, caring

Worst quality: Can get a little restless

"Don't get me wrong. Life in the Crystal Empire is wonderful, but it's become a little … predictable."

Shining Star

Shining Armor became a prince through his marriage to Princess Cadance. He was Captain of the Canterlot Royal Guard before moving to the Crystal Empire to rule alongside his wife.

Wedding Surprise

When Twilight Sparkle and Shining Armor were growing up in Canterlot, they were the very best of friends (BBBFF – Big Brother Best Friend Forever). But when Twilight Sparkle moved to Ponyville they lost touch – and when she next heard from him it was via the invitation to his wedding!

Prince Shining Armor

Occupation: Co-ruler of the Crystal Empire, former captain of the Canterlot Royal Guard

Type: Unicorn

Family: Sister Twilight Sparkle, parents Twilight Velvet and Night Light

Cutie mark: A star on a shield

Best qualities: Strong, kind, true, a great leader

Worst quality: Can be stubborn (like his little sister!)

DID YOU KNOW?
Prince Shining Armor has a soft side and has been known to cry at weddings!

"The burden of keeping Canterlot safe and secure rests squarely on my shoulders."

"Come on, gang! Are we gonna gallop, or are we gonna trot!?"

More Canterlot Ponies

Prince Blueblood

Hoity Toity

Photo Finish

Sapphire Shores

DID YOU KNOW?

Rarity looks up to glamourous High Society, who once visited her Carousel Boutique!

High Society

Fancy Pants

DID YOU KNOW?
Moon Dancer is one of Twilight Sparkle's oldest friends.

Moon Dancer

DID YOU KNOW?
These three ponies love to attend events with Fancy Pants. They agree with ALL his opinions!

Canterlot High Society

More Canterlot Ponies

Sassy Sandals

Joe

Make-up Artist

DID YOU KNOW?
Saffron Masala and her father, Corinder Cumin, run the Tasty Treat restaurant in Canterlot!

Saffron Masala

Upper Crust

Jet Set

Zesty Gourmand

Twilight Velvet

Night Light

DID YOU KNOW?
These two Canterlot residents are Twilight Sparkle's parents!

Canterlot Castle

Canterlot Castle is the grandest palace in Equestria. It has housed the royal family for many hundreds of moons. As befits a royal residence, it has many towering turrets and secret underground vaults!

From the tallest tower of the castle, the princesses can see the whole of Equestria.

Both Celestia and Luna have sumptuous suites in the castle where they sleep, rest and attend to their royal duties.

The royal kitchens are so big that they can easily provide a fabulous feast for over one thousand ponies!

There are more than one hundred rooms in Canterlot Castle!

The ballroom is used for the grandest of events, such as royal weddings and coronations. On these occasions it is decorated with fresh flowers and balloons.

The Royal Guards look after the castle, protecting the royal family from harm. They used to be led by Shining Armor.

The Royal Wedding
by Twilight Sparkle

One day I received an invitation to a wedding from Princess Celestia. Imagine my surprise to discover that it was my brother getting married – to somepony called Princess Mi Amore Cadenza. WHO IN THE HOOF WAS THAT?! I couldn't help feeling a bit sad that he hadn't told me the news himself …

My friends and I travelled by train to Canterlot. We found the city surrounded by a magical spell. Shining Armor said that a threat had been made against Canterlot – and as Captain of the Royal Guard, he was responsible for protecting it using his powerful magic. I was delighted when he asked me to be his "best mare" at the ceremony!

Next it was time to meet Shining Armor's bride to be – and I had another big surprise. The mystery princess was Cadance – a kind, caring pony who used to foal-sit for me when I was young! But Cadance had changed – she was mean, rude and demanding. I knew something very strange was going on …

I told Shining Armor my concerns and that's when I saw Cadance using a strange green magic on him. Now I knew this pony was not just mean … she was EVIL! But my brother refused to listen. He said that if I couldn't be nice to his bride, I shouldn't come to the wedding. I was upset and worried … what should I do?!

But I was soon proved right! Cadance used her magic to trap me and Spike in the caves below the castle. She revealed her dreadful plans for my brother and for Equestria. Then I found out the truth: the real Cadance was trapped underground too – she had been captured by a wicked imposter. We HAD to stop her!

Finally we escaped and ran straight to the ballroom where the wedding was taking place. Real Cadance explained that fake Cadance was in fact Queen Chrysalis, a changeling. She had been feeding off Shining Armor's love for Cadance, getting stronger and stronger!

Even Princess Celestia's magic was useless against the evil changeling queen. But then something amazing happened … When Shining Armor and Cadance's horns touched, their love was so pure and strong, it created a force powerful enough to destroy the queen and all her changeling minions! Wow!

At last the wedding could happen for real! I was so happy that my brother and Cadance were finally together. Now it was time to relax and have fun … and for me to enjoy spending time with my big brother AND my new big sister!

A New Princess

Twilight was once just a regular Unicorn (with some very powerful magic!). She became a princess after finishing a spell started by the powerful wizard Star Swirl the Bearded.

"From all of us together, together we're friends. With the marks of our destinies made one, there is magic without end!"

– Princess Twilight Sparkle's spell

Twilight's Transformation

As soon as Twilight had completed the spell, she became an Alicorn, and Princess Celestia gave her the title Princess of Friendship. The royal ruler explained that since arriving in Ponyville, Twilight had displayed the charity, compassion, devotion, integrity, optimism and leadership worthy of a true princess.

A Family Affair

The very next day, Twilight's coronation was held at Canterlot Castle. Princesses Celestia, Luna and Cadance presided over the grand occasion and Twilight's brother, Shining Armor, was so proud he even shed a tear or two ("liquid pride" as he prefers to call it).

Beautiful Ballroom

Princess Twilight Sparkle's coronation took place in the Canterlot Castle ballroom. She was accompanied by the Royal Guards and ponies carrying her "royal standard" – a special flag bearing Twilight's white and pink cutie mark.

Twilight's Tiara

As Princess of Friendship, Twilight was given a new tiara, with a six-pointed star gem at the front. It was presented to her by her number one assistant, Spike! He looked very smart in his frilled shirt and red bowtie.

Speech Time

Twilight Sparkle was pretty nervous about giving a speech in front of everypony … but it turned out just perfectly!

"A little while ago, my teacher and mentor, Princess Celestia, sent me to live in Ponyville. She sent me to study friendship, which is something I didn't really care much about.

But I wouldn't be standing here if it weren't for the friendships I've made. Each one of you taught me something about friendship, and for that, I will always be grateful. Today, I consider myself the luckiest pony in Equestria. Thank you, friends. Thank you, everypony!"

A Princess Parade

After the coronation was over, Twilight Sparkle rode on the royal chariot through the streets of Canterlot. Becoming a princess still felt like a wonderful dream …

Magical Moments

Here are some AMAZING memories from Twilight's coronation day!

Welcome to the Crystal Empire!

The Crystal Empire

Even by Equestria's standards, the Crystal Empire is a unique and magical place, created entirely from shining crystal! The Crystal Ponies can be recognised by their translucent, glistening coats and manes.

Crystal History

Long ago, the Crystal Empire was taken over by evil King Sombra, who turned it into a dark, unhappy land and enslaved the Crystal Ponies. Princesses Celestia and Luna eventually defeated him with their powerful magic, turning him to shadow and imprisoning him in the ice of the Arctic North. Good riddance!

Disappearing Trick

But King Sombra had placed a curse on the Empire, causing it to vanish for a thousand years. Once the Empire was saved, the Crystal Ponies still had no memories of their home before that time. When Sombra threatened to invade the Empire again, Celestia sent Cadance and Shining Armor to defend it.

Shining Square

The main square lies at the centre of the Empire, and is the site of the Crystal Castle. It is a busy place with many buildings, shops and restaurants. The snowflake pattern seen on the ground here spreads throughout the Empire.

The Crystal Castle

The imposing Crystal Castle is home to the rulers of the Empire. Its ultra high turrets tower above the land. During evil King Sombra's reign, the usually sparkling castle was extremely dark and foreboding.

Sparkling Spa

The spa is the most glamorous place in the whole Empire! Princess Cadance often visits for a special crystal mane scrub or hoof soak. It also features a spectacular mud bath, said to make everypony's eyes shine and their coat glow.

Super Stadium

The Crystal Empire has a huge stadium, which was built for the Equestria Games. It can seat many thousands of ponies in the grandstands. The stadium also features a special seating box for its VIP spectators, such as the princesses!

The Crystal Heart

The beautiful and powerful Crystal Heart went missing for many years, but is now back in its rightful place at the centre of the Empire. It channels the happiness of the Crystal Ponies to provide protection for all of Equestria.

The Missing Heart

While the Crystal Heart was missing, Princess Cadance and Prince Shining Armor bravely used their magic to protect the Empire from cruel King Sombra and the storms of the frozen North – but they didn't have the strength to do this for ever …

Sombra's Shadows

When Cadance's magic started to run out, King Sombra began to cover the Crystal Empire with black shadow crystals. Twilight and Spike searched the castle for the Crystal Heart, finally finding it behind a hidden staircase. But King Sombra stopped them by trapping Twilight inside a wall of shadow crystals.

Spike's Happy Heart

Twilight instructed Spike to take the Crystal Heart to Princess Cadance. King Sombra did all he could to stop Spike from accomplishing his mission, but the brave dragon passed the heart safely to the princess, who returned it to its home in the castle.

Heart of the Kingdom

Now the Crystal Heart was safe, the Crystal Ponies used its power to unleash an explosion of love and light that restored the Crystal Empire, briefly turning Cadance, Shining Armor, Twilight and her friends into Crystal Ponies. The explosion also destroyed King Sombra and his black shadow crystals.

DID YOU KNOW?
To thank Spike for his role in saving the Crystal Heart, the ponies of the Crystal Empire built a statue in his honour!

"The Crystal Heart has returned. Use the light and love within you to ensure that King Sombra does not."
– Princess Cadance

The Crystal Ponies

Sunburst

DID YOU KNOW?

Sunburst and Starlight Glimmer met at Princess Celestia's School for Gifted Unicorns. Their reunion was one of Starlight's first friendship lessons!

Stylist Ponies

Porter

Librarian

MeSSenger

Track and Field Team

Foals and Fillies

A Royal Arrival

Everypony was so excited when Princess Cadance and Prince Shining Armor announced they were having a baby. Nopony was more excited than Pinkie Pie, who was first to find out the news!

The Secret Scroll

One morning a scroll arrived at Sugarcube Corner requesting a large order of cakes and treats for a special celebration: a new royal baby would be arriving very soon! Mrs Cake told Pinkie Pie that this was TOP SECRET. Pinkie Pie was SO nervous – she wasn't sure how she would manage to keep such a massive secret!

A Royal Visit

When Shining Armor and Cadance arrived in Ponyville, Pinkie Pie thought the secret would be revealed but instead the royal couple sent her and her friends on a scavenger hunt around the whole of Ponyville. It lead them to the schoolhouse, a birth certificate and a baby's cot at the furniture store. Hmm!

A Special Announcement

Finally Twilight put two and two together, and Shining Armor and Cadance officially announced that they were expecting a baby. Twilight was thrilled about becoming an aunt – and Pinkie Pie was happy she didn't have to keep her secret any longer!

She's Here!

When the royal baby finally arrived, everypony was so excited. Twilight Sparkle and her friends rushed straight to the Crystal Empire to meet the little foal.

DID YOU KNOW?

Pinkie Pie found it so hard to keep the secret that her behaviour became EVEN stranger than usual!

DID YOU KNOW?

As a newborn, Flurry Heart could already fly and perform teleportation spells. Luckily she has plenty of skilled ponies to teach her how to use her magic carefully and wisely.

Princess Flurry Heart

Occupation: Princess of the Crystal Empire

Type: Alicorn – the first one to be born in Equestria!

Family: Parents Princess Cadance and Prince Shining Armor, aunt Princess Twilight Sparkle, great-aunt Princess Celestia

Cutie mark: Not until she's older

Best qualities: Full of magic and mischief

Worst quality: Young Princess Flurry Heart hasn't yet learnt to control her powerful magic

Raw Royal Magic!

Princess Flurry Heart is the first Alicorn ever to be born in Equestria, as Alicorn wings are usually gained by performing an incredible feat of magic. Even Princess Celestia doesn't know how powerful Princess Flurry Heart's magic will be when she grows up.

Princess Flurry Heart's Crystalling Ceremony

The "Crystalling" is a special ceremony for Crystal Empire newborns. Not only does it welcome a new baby into the world, but the love of the Crystal Ponies, gathered together to celebrate, also adds strength to the Crystal Heart.

Special Invitation

Twilight Sparkle was super excited to receive the snowflake invitation to Flurry Heart's Crystalling Ceremony. It was finally time to meet her new niece! Twilight's friends were all invited too – including Starlight Glimmer, Twilight's student.

Meeting the Princess

After catching the train to the Crystal Empire, the ponies went straight to meet the newborn foal. She was so cute – but her powerful magic was causing chaos around the Crystal Castle! Cadance wanted to cancel the Crystalling, but Celestia told her how important it was for the ceremony to take place as planned.

Crystalling Crisis

When it was time to begin the ceremony, foal-sitter Pinkie Pie handed the baby to her parents. But Flurry Heart had got so attached to Pinkie that she started to cry – and her booming wail caused the Crystal Heart to shatter into pieces. DISASTER!

Winter Wasteland

With the Crystal Heart in pieces, the Crystal Empire was left unprotected from the Arctic North's winter storms. Thick snow clouds moved in and even Rainbow Dash couldn't clear them away. As Celestia and Luna used their magic to keep the storm clouds at bay, Twilight and her friends raced to the library to find a spell to restore the Crystal Heart.

Light and Love

Luckily Starlight Glimmer's friend Sunburst had an idea. Together, Twilight, Starlight, Celestia and Luna would cast their powerful magic on the Crystal Heart, while Sunburst, Cadance and Shining Armor would carry out the Crystalling. The light and love of the Crystal Ponies was focussed into a single crystal, which Sunburst merged with the Crystal Heart. The resulting magic restored the Heart and saved the Empire. PHEW!

115

Baby Flurry Heart's Best Bits!

Welcome to the world ... Princess Flurry Heart's proud parents, relatives and friends gathered round her crystal crib.

A winged wonder! Baby Flurry Heart is the first Alicorn baby ever to be born in Equestria.

Supersonic sneeze! This baby's sneeze is SO powerful that it blasted through several ceilings!

Flurry Heart just ADORES Pinkie Pie, her favourite foal-sitter!

Cry baby! Separated from Pinkie Pie, Flurry Heart has the biggest tantrum EVER!

Cadance and Shining Armor named their daughter Flurry Heart to commemorate how the Crystal Heart was restored and the Empire saved from eternal winter.

Baby Flurry Heart and her new Crystaller and magic advisor, Sunburst.

Everypony – including Baby Flurry Heart – turned briefly into a Crystal Pony during the magical Crystalling ceremony!

Photo Finish

Here are some super-special photos of Princess Flurry Heart's Crystalling ... along with some of the other dramatic events of the day!

Welcome to the Everfree Forest!

The Everfree Forest

The mysterious Everfree Forest is found on the outskirts of Ponyville. It's home to some very strange creatures and plants that don't need ponies to look after them – unlike the rest of Equestria.

Search For the Elements

Twilight and her friends first ventured into the forest in their search for the Elements of Harmony. Everypony was scared – even plucky Applejack admitted: "It ain't natural; folks say it don't work the same as the rest of Equestria!"

Fluttershy's Fears

Fluttershy lives in a little cottage on the edge of the forest. She loves all animals … but she's wary of going too far into the forest. Sometimes, late at night, she hears strange howls, growls and moans coming from the depths of the woods …

Pinkie's Pool

One day Pinkie Pie ventured into the forest to look for a magical pond she'd heard about in a nursery rhyme. When she stepped into the "mirror pool", a second Pinkie Pie appeared, and soon Pinkie clones were creating havoc across Ponyville – until Twilight returned them to the pool!

Everfree Friends

Although almost everypony fears the forest, there are some creatures who enjoy living among the trees. Zecora is one happy resident and uses the forest plants in her special medicines and potions.

Poison Joke Japes

Strange things grow in the Everfree Forest, including a pretty blue flower known as Poison Joke. This plant may look innocent but it caused very strange things to happen to the ponies ...

Twilight Sparkle's horn became soft and wobbly, and covered in blue spots.

Rainbow Dash's wings were turned upside down, making her crash constantly.

Applejack shrank to a tiny size.

Rarity's mane, coat and tail became frizzled like a mop.

Pinkie Pie's tongue was swollen and covered in blue spots.

Fluttershy's voice became deep, like a male pony.

Luckily the effects of Poison Joke wore off when the ponies took a herbal bath!

DID YOU KNOW?

It's very easy to get lost in the Everfree Forest. The paths twist and turn and sometimes seem to have a mind of their own!

Creatures of the Everfree Forest

Zecora

Occupation: Herbalist
Type: Zebra
Family: A mystery!
Cutie mark: Grey spiral
Best qualities Wise, calm, knowledgeable
Worst quality: Can seem a little frightening when you don't know her!

The Wise Healer

Zecora is a wise and mysterious zebra who lives in a hut in the Everfree Forest. She has become a valuable friend of the ponies, often sharing her knowledge of magical medicines with them. With golden bangles around her neck and a spiky mane, Zecora looks as exotic as her spells and almost always speaks in rhyme:

*"Now, Apple Bloom,
do not be silly.*

*You are always welcome,
my little filly.*

*With each mistake
you learn something new,*

Growing up into a better you."

Cerberus

You'll get a shock if you bump into this three-headed dog in the deep dark woods! Cerberus is responsible for guarding the gates of Tartarus, a place where dark, mythical creatures are imprisoned. His three heads mean he has extra eyes to watch out for any escapees.

DID YOU KNOW?

Like most dogs, Cerberus can't resist a tummy rub or a game of fetch!

122

The Ursas

The Ursas are huge magical bears. Their fur looks like the night sky, with bright stars making a constellation on their big translucent bodies. Ursa Major is an adult, while Ursa Minor is a young cub.

Bear Boasting

Trixie, a boastful Unicorn, once told everypony that she defeated an Ursa Major that was attacking the village of Hoofington. Snips and Snails went into the Everfree Forest, hoping to find another one, so they could see Trixie repeat her feat!

They did find one – and it chased them back to Ponyville. Trixie was powerless to help them and had to admit she had lied about her exploits. With Ponyville under threat from the enormous Ursa, clever Twilight Sparkle was able to calm the bear down with a magical lullaby and a giant bottle of milk. It turned out that the creature was an Ursa Minor not an Ursa Major … Phew!

DID YOU KNOW?

The gigantic Ursa Major is the biggest creature in the whole of Equestria!

"I can't, I never have. No one can vanquish an Ursa Major. I just made the whole story up to make me look better."
– Trixie

123

More Creatures of the Everfree Forest

Timberwolf

Timberwolves are unique creatures whose bodies are made up of logs, twigs and leaves. They have glowing green eyes which shine menacingly in the dark. When these wolves howl, it's a sign that the mystical Zap apples are about to start their super-fast, magical growing season.

DID YOU KNOW?
Spike once wandered into the forest and was attacked by Timberwolves. Luckily Applejack was on hand to help him!

DID YOU KNOW?
The best way to escape a Timberwolf is to break it into bits. But this wily wolf will soon piece itself back together again!

Cockatrice

What do you get if you cross a chicken and a snake? A cockatrice! This funny-looking creature is known to hang out in the Everfree Forest. It looks a bit silly, but actually has some serious powers. By staring into a victim's eyes, the cockatrice can turn anypony into stone.

DID YOU KNOW?
Using her impressive "Stare", Fluttershy has the power to force a cockatrice to reverse its stony spell.

Parasprites

Parasprites are insect-like creatures that swarm together and will eat their way through ANYTHING. One day, kind Fluttershy came across a single parasprite and decided to adopt it. She didn't know that one parasprite can create another by coughing it up (ew!). Soon the ponies had to deal with a huge hungry swarm …

Cragadile

Cragadiles live in the swamps deep in the Everfree Forest and are rarely seen by anypony. These cranky creatures look a bit like a crocodile but their tough skin is made from rocks.

DID YOU KNOW?

Wise Zecora has something to say about parasprites: "Tales of crops and harvests consumed. If these creatures are in Ponyville, you're doomed!"

Manticore

A manticore has the body of a lion, the tail of a scorpion and a pair of dragon-like wings. When Twilight Sparkle and her friends bumped into a manticore as they searched for the Elements of Harmony, it seemed very fierce – but it became friendly once Fluttershy had pulled a large thorn from its paw.

125

Secrets of the Forest

It's not just strange creatures that live deep in the Everfree Forest – there are some truly mysterious places waiting to be discovered too ...

The Castle of the Two Sisters

This ancient castle is where Princess Celestia and Princess Luna lived over a thousand years ago, long before taking up residence in Canterlot Castle. Once a grand and majestic place, it is now empty and spooky.

Friendship Findings

When Twilight Sparkle first came to Ponyville, she and her new friends travelled to the castle to retrieve the Elements of Harmony, which they needed in order to destroy Nightmare Moon and save Equestria from eternal night (and an eternal nightmare!). The friends discovered that each of them represented an Element of Harmony, and that their friendship would protect Equestria.

The Tree of Harmony

This magical tree, located in the Cave of Harmony, deep in the Everfree Forest, is the source of the Elements of Harmony. Princesses Celestia and Luna discovered it many years ago, when they lived in the castle nearby. The princesses took the powerful Elements and used them to defeat the villainous Discord. Then they hid the Elements safely in the castle … which is where Twilight and her friends later discovered them.

The Elements of Harmony

The ponies had only just met each other when they embarked on an adventure that would change their lives – and the future of Equestria – FOR EVER!

The Adventure Begins ...

After Princess Celestia was pony-napped by Nightmare Moon on the eve of the Summer Sun Celebration, Twilight Sparkle knew that only she could help her mentor and friend. Twilight discovered that the one source of magic that could defeat Nightmare Moon was the Elements of Harmony, located in the ruins of the "ancient castle of the royal pony sisters" in the Everfree Forest.

In It Together

During the dangerous journey to the ruined castle, Twilight's friends each demonstrated a wonderful quality. These qualities were honesty, kindness, laughter, generosity and loyalty.

The Magic of Friendship

When they eventually reached the castle, the friends found five stone orbs that they thought were the Elements of Harmony. But cruel Nightmare Moon destroyed the orbs and the friends thought all was lost. But then Twilight realised that the five Elements were represented by her five friends …

In promising Twilight that she would be safe, Applejack displayed honesty.

Fluttershy helped the fierce Manticore who was in pain and showed him kindness.

Rainbow Dash put aside selfish desires to think of her friends, demonstrating loyalty.

Rarity helped an unhappy river serpent by giving him her beautiful tail, displaying generosity.

Pinkie Pie helped all her friends overcome their fear with laughter.

Rainbow Resolution

When all these Elements came together, they kindled something special in Twilight Sparkle's heart. The moment Twilight realised these amazing ponies were true friends, the sixth Element of Harmony was revealed: MAGIC! This was Twilight's own Element. The Elements then appeared as necklaces on each of her friends, and as a tiara on Twilight Sparkle. A rainbow-coloured blast of magic appeared that destroyed Nightmare Moon and returned her to her original form of Princess Luna.

DID YOU KNOW?
The Elements of Harmony are said to be "the most powerful magic known to Ponydom".

The History of Harmony

Strange Plants

The Elements of Harmony were separated from the Tree of Harmony for many years, but the tree still controlled everything that grew in the Everfree Forest. When princesses Celestia and Luna disappeared, mysterious black weeds started to grow throughout Equestria – and Twilight Sparkle realised that the strange plants were connected in some way to the tree …

A Near Miss

Twilight and her friends finally found the Tree of Harmony deep in the forest. They could see it was dying. Twilight Sparkle realised that they needed to return the Elements of Harmony to the tree in order to save it. Although they would miss having such powerful magic, they knew that their friendship would remain as strong as ever.

"The Elements of Harmony did bring us together. But it isn't the Elements that will keep us connected. It's our friendship. And it's more important and more powerful than any magic." – Twilight Sparkle

Back in Bloom

With the Elements back in their rightful place, the choking black weeds disappeared and the tree glowed with magic. Suddenly princesses Celestia and Luna reappeared! The ponies learned that the weeds had grown from seeds that tricksy Discord had planted many thousands of years ago. Once a pest, always a pest!

DID YOU KNOW?

When the tree was back to full health, it produced a mysterious chest with six keyholes. Twilight would need to find six keys to open it.

Cloudsdale

Welcome to the cloud city in the sky! Magnificent Cloudsdale is a truly unique place, sitting on a huge fluffy cloud. It's much bigger than it looks and nothing stays the same for long as the clouds move through the skies above Equestria.

Pegasi Place

Only Pegasus ponies can live in Cloudsdale, as you need wings to get around. When Twilight Sparkle became an Alicorn princess (and mastered her new wings!), she was able to fly up to the clouds with Rainbow Dash and the other Pegasus ponies. Non-winged ponies can pay a visit by hopping in a hot-air balloon.

Weather Ways

All of the weather in Equestria is created in Cloudsdale's weather factory. This amazing factory contains special departments for raindrop design, snowflake creation, cloud control and even rainbow pools.

The Cloudseum

This impressive up-in-the-air stadium is ENORMOUS. It hosts Cloudsdale's biggest flying events such as the Best Young Flyer Competition. Many hundreds of Pegasus ponies can gather on the cloud stands to watch the races and cheer on their favourite competitor. Most Pegasus ponies are very competitive ... none more so than Rainbow Dash!

Wonderful Wonderbolts

The Wonderbolts are an elite squad of Pegasus ponies who perform aerial acrobatics and flying demonstrations. These fantastic flyers have talent, speed and more – enough to impress even Rainbow Dash!

Best Young Flyer

Rainbow Dash was determined to win the Best Young Flyer Competition and secure the first prize: a day of flying with the Wonderbolts. When she stopped to rescue Rarity, who had lost control of her magical wings, she thought she'd blown her chances.

But while rescuing Rarity, Rainbow Dash also saved the Wonderbolts Soarin, Spitfire and Misty Fly from airborne disaster – and in the process triggered a rare Sonic Rainboom. Rainbow Dash won the competition AND the best prize of all – spending the day flying with her heroes!

Tough Training

Rainbow Dash was desperate to join the Wonderbolts, so she was over the moon to be accepted into the Reserves. Aspiring Wonderbolts have to endure some seriously tough training. Only the best young flyers make it into – and graduate from – the Wonderbolts Academy!

DID YOU KNOW?

The Wonderbolts always look super cool in their matching uniforms of blue suits with gold lightning patterns and mirrored goggles.

Life Lessons

Rainbow Dash was so confident in her flying abilities that she thought she'd breeze through the Wonderbolts training. But it was much harder than she had realised … When her friends almost got badly hurt during a training exercise, Rainbow Dash decided to tell the captain, Spitfire, that she didn't want to be part of the squad any more:

"No disrespect, ma'am, but there's a big difference between pushing yourself as hard as you can and just being reckless. And if being reckless is what it means to be a Wonderbolt, then I don't want any part of it."

Luckily Spitfire agreed with her and made some changes. Rainbow Dash did eventually become part of the squad!

Spitfire

Spitfire is a female Pegasus pony and the captain of the Wonderbolts. This fearless flyer has earned the respect of her team for being tough-talking but fair.

Soarin

Soarin is second-in-command and issues orders when Spitfire is away from the squad.

Fleetfoot

Fleetfoot is another key member of the squad. She was given the nickname "Flatfoot" on her first day as a Wonderbolt but it hasn't held her back in the slightest!

Blaze

Blaze is a super-fast flyer and can be identified by her distinctive orange mane and tail.

The squad also includes Wave Chill, Wind Waker, Sun Chaser, Silver Zoom, Misty Fly and Lightning Streak.

Wonderbolts Academy

Found high in the skies above Equestria, the Wonderbolts Academy is the training school for future Wonderbolt flyers. Cadets come from all over Equestria, dreaming of one day joining the legendary flying squad.

Historic Halls

The Wonderbolts were originally formed by General Firefly, who was so impressed by the amazing aerial acrobatics of Princess Celestia's E.U.P. (Earth, Unicorn, Pegasus) Guard that he set up a new elite flying squad. Many an adventurous young Pegasus pony has dreamt of taking up residence in the inspiring surroundings of the academy!

Living Together

In addition to its famous outdoor training facilities, the academy has classrooms, a library, a dormitory and locker room. The academy prides itself on nurturing the qualities of patience, tolerance and respect in its cadets – to excel here, you need to be able to get along with everypony!

Challenging Training

Outside, the cadets are put through their paces by experienced and dedicated drill instructors Fast Clip, Whiplash and Spitfire. They push their students hard – they know not everypony is cut out to be a Wonderbolt! Spitfire is also the Wonderbolts team captain, and one of Rainbow Dash's heroes.

DID YOU KNOW?

The Wonderbolts' special motto is "Altius volantis", which means "soaring higher"!

DID YOU KNOW?

On her first attempt, Rainbow Dash managed to recover from the Dizzitron in an impressive six seconds!

On Your Marks ...

The cadets' training regime includes a tricky obstacle course (testing agility and navigation skills), flag drill (hunting and retrieving coloured flags), barrel rolls, wing lifts and the dreaded Dizzitron, which spins a cadet round at top speed to test how fast they can recover.

Homes on High

With the exception of Fluttershy, Pegasus ponies are at their most comfortable up in the air, so Cloudsdale is the perfect home ...

Flutter Family

Unlike their daughter Fluttershy, Mr and Mrs Shy live high in the clouds. Mrs Shy is a gardener and Mr Shy is a retired weather factory worker and cloud collector. They are even more timid and soft-spoken than Fluttershy – in fact they consider her to be the bold one of the family!

Zephyr Breeze

Zephyr Breeze is the son of Mr and Mrs Shy and Fluttershy's younger brother. Unlike his parents, Zephyr is a bit of a wanderer and has lived in lots of different places in Equestria, trying many different jobs. He finds it hard to stay put!

DID YOU KNOW?

Zephyr Breeze has a crush on Rainbow Dash – but she thinks he is very annoying!

Weather Workers

Hard-working Pegasus ponies Sunshower, Open Skies, Clear Skies and Fluffy Clouds help to keep the weather on track. In the winter months they move clouds from the weather factory to the skies above Ponyville. When the sunshine and rain have been out, it's their job to send in some beautiful rainbows.

Cloudsdale Cheer Ponies

Spring Step and Lilac Sky are two lively Pegasus ponies who act as cheerleaders for the Equestria Games and other competitive aerial events. These perky Pegasus ponies perform all manner of tumbles, twists, leaps and cheers.

P for Pegasus

The royal guards, also known as the Protective Pony Platoons or E.U.P. (Earth, Unicorn, Pegasus) do an important job protecting princesses Celestia, Luna and the rest of the royal family – and they include lots of strong Pegasus ponies. They work alongside Earth ponies and Unicorns as bodyguards, ceremonial guards, soldiers and chauffeurs.

More Cloudsdale Ponies

Bully Pony

Mail Carrier

Weather Workers

Trainers

Wonderbolt Instructors

Whiplash

Fast Clip

Wonderbolt Cadets

Orange Swirl

Thunderlane

Pizelle

Wild Fire

Midnight Strike

Crazy For Cloudsdale

Cloudsdale is a truly unique place – there's no other location in Equestria quite like it. Here are some fascinating facts about everypony's favourite cloud city ...

Lots of plants and flowers grow in Cloudsdale, despite it being made from clouds. Fluttershy's mum has very green hooves and ponies flock from miles around to see her beautiful blooms!

Once, a weather factory malfunction (caused by none other than Rainbow Dash!), caused a HUGE snowball to fall on Ponyville, kicking off an early winter. Brrrr!

There are lots of different types of clouds, including cirrus clouds (the wispy ones), stratus clouds (grey fog clouds covering the whole sky) and alto clouds (the stormy ones). Each cloud is truly unique!

Each year the Pegasus ponies take water up from the reservoir in Ponyville to use in the Weather Factory. They do this by making an enormous tornado to funnel up the water!

Inside the weather factory, one very skilled pony has the important job of checking that every individual snowflake is just perfect!

The Rest of Equestria

Magnificent Manehattan

Welcome to Manehattan, the busiest, most bustling city in Equestria. There's something for everypony in this cool metropolis ... shops, restaurants, theatres and much, much more.

Sweeping Skyline

When you approach Manehattan, you can't help but be impressed by the skyline bursting with skyscrapers and statues. Lots of important ponies live and have their businesses in Manehattan – if you're a career pony, it's the place to come!

Ocean Views

Manehattan is situated right on the edge of Equestria, by the Celestial Ocean. One way of travelling to the city is by boat. You can also take boat trips around the city to see some of the famous sights, including the Mare Statue!

Applejack the City Pony

When Applejack was a young filly, she packed a bag and set off to discover her destiny in Manehattan, staying with Aunt and Uncle Orange. Applejack met everypony in Manehattan high society and experienced fine dining (she didn't like the TINY portions!), but she felt very homesick and decided to return to Sweet Apple Acres.

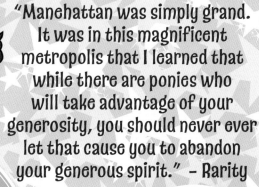

"Manehattan was simply grand. It was in this magnificent metropolis that I learned that while there are ponies who will take advantage of your generosity, you should never ever let that cause you to abandon your generous spirit." – Rarity

DID YOU KNOW?

Cheese Sandwich (Pinkie Pie's rival party-organiser!) comes from Manehattan. He was glad to move away from the big city, preferring to be a wandering party pony.

DID YOU KNOW?

The quickest way to get across Manehattan is to jump in one of the city's many yellow taxis, pulled by a helpful driver!

Dream Destinations

Rarity LOVES everything about Manehattan, from the fabulous fashions to the wonderful shows held in the theatre district, Bridleway. Rarity once took her best friends to the city for Fashion Week. Although the trip had its ups and downs, the "hotel chic" designs that her friends helped Rarity to create in their hotel room won Rarity first prize in the final fashion show!

More Manehattan Ponies

Prim Hemline

Suri Polomare

Miss Pommel

Coloratura

Buried Lede

Hat
Merchant

Plaid
Stripes

Fashion
Ponies

Fashion Best Bits!

Design disaster … When Rarity's friends demand that she use ALL their ideas to create new outfits, the result is one big MESS!

Applejack knows her Stetson suits her better than this OTT princess gown …

Medieval chic … The CMCs take to the stage wearing fabulous medieval frocks in a theatrical attempt to earn their cutie marks.

Nopony is more glamorous than Rarity!

Discord makes a surprising fashion statement ...

... followed by another!

Camouflage chic!

Pinkie Pie tries to outdo her party-planner rival Cheese Sandwich with the ultimate party outfit ...

Dragon chic!

Sweet Home Appleloosa

The small town of Appleloosa couldn't be more different from big Manehattan! This happy homestead is in the central west of Equestria, south of the Everfree Forest and north of the mysterious Badlands.

Applejack's Family Ties

As you might guess from its name, Applejack has relatives in Appleloosa! Her cousin Braeburn lives in the town with his family, and Applejack once delivered a very special apple tree, named Bloomberg, to add to the town's orchard.

Stampeding Stand-Off

When the first ponies arrived in Appleloosa, they decided to plant a big orchard so that they could live off the apple produce. Unfortunately, they planted it on the site of the stampeding ground of a large herd of buffalo, who had lived in that area for many years.

The buffalo were furious and this led to a huge fight, with the ponies throwing apple pies and the buffalo using all their brute strength! Thankfully, after an apple pie hit Chief Thunderhooves in the face and he realised how delicious apples could be, they reached a compromise: the ponies kept their orchard but built a road through it so that the buffalos could continue to stampede as usual.

DID YOU KNOW?

The town includes a saloon called the Salt Block, as well as a clock tower and a stage for musical performances.

DID YOU KNOW?

The easiest way to reach Appleloosa is to catch the train. The tracks run right through the heart of town, handy for visits and deliveries!

Rocking Rodeo

Each year in Appleloosa a rodeo is held. The rodeo is full of exciting events such as barrel racing, roping contests, rodeo clowning and a steeplechase. It's one of the highlights of Applejack's year.

151

The Good Ponyfolk of Appleloosa

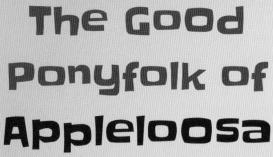

Many of the ponies who live in Appleloosa are related to Applejack. Here's the lowdown on some of the community's most familiar faces ...

Braeburn

Occupation: Farmer, orchard manager

Type: Earth pony

Family: A huge extended family, including Applejack, Apple Bloom, Big Mac and Granny Smith

Cutie mark: A shiny red apple

Best qualities: Friendly, hardworking, determined

Worst quality: Stubborn (a bit of an Apple family trait!)

"Hey there. Welcome to AAAAAAA-pple-LOO-sa!"

"Cousin Applejack, mind yer manners. You have yet ta introduce me to your compadres!"

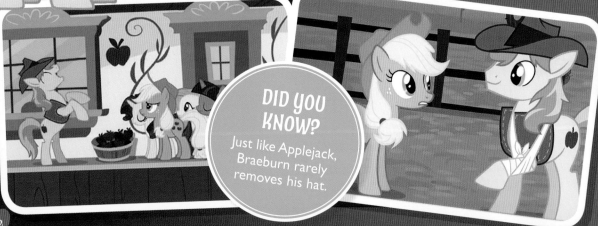

DID YOU KNOW?
Just like Applejack, Braeburn rarely removes his hat.

Sheriff Silverstar

Occupation: Leader of Appleloosa

Type: Earth pony

Family: A mystery!

Cutie mark: A shining silver star

Best qualities: Law-abiding, respectable

Worst quality: Doesn't like to be proved wrong. After all, he's the boss!

DID YOU KNOW?

Sheriff Silverstar is very proud of his moustache. He combs it each morning to make sure it's curled at the ends.

"An' we Appleloosans say you'd better bring yer best, 'cause we'll be ready and waitin'."

Chief Thunderhooves

Occupation: Chief of the buffalo tribe

Type: Buffalo

Family: A mystery!

Cutie mark: None

Best qualities: A strong leader, wise, loyal

Worst quality: Finds it hard to ever believe he is wrong

DID YOU KNOW?

The chief weighs as much as twenty full-grown ponies. When he stampedes, the ground shakes. It's no wonder his name is "Thunderhooves"!

Little Strongheart

Occupation: Unofficial second-in-command to Chief Thunderhooves

Type: Buffalo

Family: A mystery!

Cutie mark: None

Best qualities: Brave, resourceful, spirited

Worst quality: Can be fierce

DID YOU KNOW?

All members of the buffalo tribe wear their headpiece and feathers with pride. It's a very important part of their culture!

Meet the Pie Family

The Pies live on a rock farm to the west of Appleloosa. They are very dedicated to their work, digging rocks out of the ground. Here's all you need to know about Pinkie Pie's surprising family ...

Igneous Rock Pie (aka Pa Pie)

Occupation: Rock farmer

Type: Earth pony

Family: Husband to Ma Pie, father to Pinkie Pie, Maud Pie, Limestone Pie and Marble Pie

Cutie mark: A chisel

Best qualities: Hard-working, loyal, dedicated

Worst quality: A pony of few words, he can find it hard to describe what he's feeling

Cloudy Quartz (aka Ma Pie)

Occupation: Rock farmer

Type: Earth pony

Family: Wife to Pa Pie, mother to Pinkie Pie, Maud Pie, Limestone Pie and Marble Pie

Cutie mark: Three rocks

Best qualities: Kind, loyal, caring

Worst quality: Can be a little stuck in her ways

DID YOU KNOW?

Ma Pie and Pa Pie have been married for a very long time. They were chosen for each other by a "pairing stone".

Marble Pie

Occupation: Helper on the family rock farm

Type: Earth pony

Family: Little sister of Pinkie Pie, Limestone Pie and Marble Pie

Cutie mark: Three purple marbles

Best qualities: Friendly, helpful, modest

Worst quality: Can be shy

Maud Pie

Occupation: Helper on the family rock farm, studying to be a geologist

Type: Earth pony

Family: Sister to Pinkie Pie, Limestone Pie and Marble Pie. Maud Pie is the second eldest sister.

Cutie mark: No one knows as Maud always wears her favourite teal dress. It's sure to be something rock-related given her love of all things stony

Best qualities: Studious, loyal, calm

Worst quality: Can be rather too rock-focused!

DID YOU KNOW?
Limestone Pie and Marble Pie are SO close that they can "talk" to each other by blinking and nodding.

Limestone Pie

Occupation: Helper on the family rock farm

Type: Earth pony

Family: Big sister to Pinkie Pie, Limestone Pie and Marble Pie

Cutie mark: A lime and two stones

Best qualities: Feisty, friendly, loyal

Worst qualities: Can be bossy and bad-tempered, especially when she's protecting Holder's Boulder, the huge grey rock located on the farm!

More of Equestria

So you've explored Ponyville, visited Canterlot and the Crystal Empire, and braved the Everfree Forest ... Now here's the lowdown on the rest of Equestria's amazing locations!

Dodge Junction

Just like its neighbour Appleoosa, Dodge Junction is located in the middle of the desert and has a train track running through it. It's home to lots of hard-working Earth ponies and has a saloon, ranches and shops. But unlike Appleoosa, which is known for its apples, Dodge Junction is famed for its cherry orchards. These orchards are managed by Cherry Jubilee, a super-friendly Earth pony.

DID YOU KNOW?

Applejack once travelled to Dodge Junction for some time out after her disappointing performance in the rodeo. But hardworking Applejack doesn't really "do" holiday — instead she helped with the cherry harvest!

DID YOU KNOW?

Rarity plans to open a boutique in Fillydelphia. She has her heart set on dressing fashionable fillies across the whole of Equestria.

Fillydelphia

Fillydelphia is almost as big as Manehattan, and both cities believe that they are the best! Fillydelphia is home to dragons as well as ponies. The dragon and pony residents live in separate parts of town, which is lucky as these dragons aren't always careful where they breathe their fire!

Las Pegasus

This premier party destination is another cloud city in the sky, although it's much smaller than Cloudsdale. Known for its bright lights and buzzing atmosphere, Las Pegasus attracts fun-loving ponies from around Equestria. Its streets and squares are full of shows, fairground rides and amazing sights.

When Applejack and Fluttershy visited Las Pegasus they were taken aback by the bright lights and loud noises, and quickly realised that Pinkie Pie or Rainbow Dash would enjoy the place a little more than they did! After a few days they were very glad to return to peaceful Ponyville!

DID YOU KNOW?
You don't need wings to enjoy the sights and delights of Las Pegasus. Bridges link each location so everypony can explore and have a good time.

Rainbow Falls

This magical place is surrounded by rainbows that descend like waterfalls – hence the village's name! Due to its location high up in the mountains, most of the visitors are Pegasus ponies, including some who come to practise their aerial relays. The qualifying races for the last Equestria Games were held here. Rainbow Dash and the Ponyville team were delighted to qualify!

More of Equestria

Froggy Bottom Bog

This marshy area is located to the south of the Everfree Forest. Filled with swampy ground and pools of stagnant water, it's a dangerous place for anypony to venture as it's easy to get sucked into the swamps.

One day, animal-loving Fluttershy travelled to Froggy Bottom to release some frog friends. Her pony pals suspected she might lose her way so they went after her … only to find her safe and well. But then an ENORMOUS hydra appeared behind them, and the ponies only just managed to escape its four heads, with poor Spike having to be rescued from a super stinky swamp!

DID YOU KNOW?
It is said that ponies have ventured into Froggy Bottom and never returned … Eek!

Dragon Lands

This dry and mountainous area is home to hundreds of dragons. Each year, dragons come here from all over Equestria to take part in a series of challenges to see who is strongest and noisiest. Spike decided to compete one year but soon realised how rude and mean most dragons are. He decided he was better off in Equestria with his pony friends!

DID YOU KNOW?

To become Dragon Lord, a dragon must win the deadly "Gauntlet of Fire" trial. Spike was relieved when his friend, kind Princess Ember, beat the rest of the cruel dragon competitors and was declared leader.

White Tail Woods

White Tail Woods is located to the west of Ponyville and the Everfree Forest. During the annual "Running of the Leaves" race, the ponies gallop through the woods at top speed to knock the leaves from the trees ready for winter. One year, Applejack and Rainbow Dash were so busy being competitive with each other that they forgot all about the leaves. Luckily Princess Celestia was there to remind them what true friendship is about … then to send them back to finish clearing the trees.

Ghastly Gorge

The Ghastly Gorge is a deep valley which runs through the centre of Equestria. It has steep, rocky walls and a stream passing through it. Watch out for the Quarry Eels – these sharp-toothed critters are not at all friendly and they eat pretty much anything … Yikes!

Daring Do's Dazzling Deeds

Some ponies can never stay in one place for long. Daring Do is one of the most adventurous ponies in Equestria – she has travelled the length and breadth of the land, exploring long-lost temples and writing about her adventures in a series of bestselling books.

No.1 Fan

When Rainbow Dash was in hospital, receiving treatment for a broken wing, Twilight Sparkle gave her one of Daring Do's books. Although Dash would never have described herself as a reader, she was soon completely wrapped up in Daring Do's tales.

Daring Do (also known as A.K. Yearling)

Occupation: Treasure hunter, explorer, adventurer, author

Type: Pegasus pony

Family: A mystery!

Cutie mark: A compass

Best qualities: Brave, fearless, fun-loving, fierce

Worst quality: Can't always be relied upon as you never know when she'll be on the move!

DID YOU KNOW?

Although Daring Do describes herself as a "loner", even she needs a little help sometimes. When Rainbow Dash helped to free her from a trap, the two ponies formed a strong bond.

As a journalist, Trenderhoof roams around Equestria on the lookout for sensational stories and groovy gossip. According to Rarity (who's a huge fan), Trenderhoof is single-hoovedly responsible for making Las Pegasus THE party destination.

Travelling Trenderhoof

Apple of His Eye

When Trenderhoof visited Ponyville to attend the Ponyville Days festival, Rarity decided to show him the sights. She was determined to impress Trenderhoof – but the pony who caught his eye was none other than … Applejack! Despite his best attempts to impress her, Applejack was not won over and thought he was nothing but a smooth-talker.

DID YOU KNOW?
Trenderhoof told Applejack that he would like to come and live with her on Sweet Apple Acres! Applejack politely but firmly turned him down.

Trenderhoof

Occupation: Journalist, travel writer

Type: Unicorn

Family: A mystery!

Cutie mark: Two diamonds marked by two large crosses

Best qualities: Curious, determined, fashionable

Worst quality: Can't always see what's right in front of his nose … like spotting Rarity's crush on him OR Applejack's total lack of interest!

Mighty Iron Will

This super-confident minotaur travels throughout Equestria, delivering assertiveness training to anypony who needs it (and a few who don't!). He claims his methods will work on anypony, absolutely no exceptions!

Fluttershy the Bold

Iron Will's methods may have worked TOO well when he demonstrated them on timid Fluttershy – her aggressive new behaviour drove all her friends away! Luckily it wasn't long before Fluttershy returned to her usual gentle self – but she still found the strength to refuse Iron Will's demands to be paid a fee for his unwelcome services!

Iron Will

Occupation: Self-help guru and motivational speaker

Type: Minotaur

Family: A mystery!

Cutie mark: None

Best qualities: Self-belief, determination

Worst quality: He has a very high opinion of himself!

"Iron Will is so confident that you will be 100% satisfied with Iron Will's assertiveness techniques, that if you are not 100% satisfied, you. Pay. Nothing."

The Dark Side

Friend or Foe?

Sometimes it's as clear as a sunny day in Ponyville who is a good guy and who is a bad guy. But other times, it's a bit mixed up ... more like a misty day in Cloudsdale.

The Mare in the Moon

As the villainous alter ego of Princess Luna, Nightmare Moon was a wicked mare of darkness, full of jealousy and rage. She was so powerful that she could turn her entire form into mist. She could also harness lightning and appear in ponies' dreams. Vengeful Nightmare Moon had planned to banish her older sister, Celestia, and unleash an eternal night on Equestria.

DID YOU KNOW?

Princess Luna dressed up as Nightmare Moon in order to scare the young foals on "Nightmare Night". The foals love to be scared on this one special night and asked Princess Luna to do the same each year!

Dark Powers

Princess Celestia knew that only the powerful Elements of Harmony could break the spell that had transformed her sister Luna into vengeful Nightmare Moon. Thank goodness Twilight Sparkle and her friends were able to harness the magic of friendship, using the Elements of Harmony to banish Nightmare Moon and bringing back kind Princess Luna to rule over Equestria alongside her sister.

"I'm not playing fair? Perhaps we haven't met. I'm Discord, spirit of chaos and disharmony. Hello?"

DID YOU KNOW?

Discord was once imprisoned in a stone statue by princesses Celestia and Luna. Many years later, Twilight used her magic to turn him to stone again.

Dastardly Discord

Discord is a Draconequus – a rare combination of many kinds of animal. With a dragon's tail, an eagle's claw, a horse's neck and two different horns, Discord looks mismatched, so it's no surprise that he represents the spirit of disharmony. Formerly a foe, he is now a friend to the ponies.

Best Behaviour

Gentle Fluttershy was the first to recognise the good in Discord and show him true friendship. Nowadays Discord tries his best to be good – he sees the worth in relationships that are kind and a little more predictable. However, he still LOVES mischief and if there's trouble in Equestria, it's likely that Discord will be found nearby!

Rogue Royals

♥ ♥

Celestia, Luna, Shining Armor, Cadance ... all of these royals rule with kindness and strength. But there are other royals who play by their own rules and only have their own interests at heart ...

The Changeling Queen

With the power to take the form of another being, Queen Chrysalis is as scary as any villain. She is cruel, clever and arrogant, and has the power to feed off everypony's emotions. When Chrysalis disguised herself as Princess Cadance on the day of her wedding to Shining Armor, it took all of the real Cadance's love for her future husband to defeat the evil changeling queen.

Charmless Changelings

Queen Chrysalis's minions are horrible creatures, capable of changing their form and appearance. Most of the time they look like a cross between a pony and an insect, with huge eyes and jagged wings. One small changeling called Thorax proved an exception to the rule. Having been shown kindness by Spike, brave Thorax dared to reveal his yearning for friendship.

The Dark King

Long ago, King Sombra was the evil ruler of the Crystal Empire. His heart was as black as night, and he put his subjects in chains. He was defeated and banished to the icy and barren land north of Equestria. But then he escaped, and put a curse on the Crystal Empire that made it – and all its ponies – vanish. Once the Empire reappeared a thousand moons later, Princess Celestia knew King Sombra would return soon as well.

Metal Warrior

King Sombra is always ready for battle and is clad from mane to tail in armour. He has sharp fangs and his Unicorn horn glows red when he uses his magic. He is a truly terrifying sight to behold!

DID YOU KNOW?
Whenever Sombra is around and using his dark magic, spiky black crystals appear.

Crystal Slaves

The poor pony residents of the Crystal Empire can remember little about the years they were ruled by King Sombra, as he used his magic to control their minds and bodies. It was only when Celestia – and later Twilight – managed to overpower him that the ponies returned to their sparkling selves and could live happy lives once more.

Tricksters and Tyrants

Some creatures are bad to the bone ... and others are just a bit slippery! The Mane Six have come across most kinds of ponies and creatures – and the magic of friendship has certainly been put to the test.

Terrifying Tirek

Lord Tirek was an evil centaur who escaped from Tartarus, where he had been imprisoned. With Discord's help, he stole the magic of all the ponies of Equestria – the Earth ponies, Unicorns and Pegasus ponies. But he would not stop until he had the magic of the royal Alicorns as well.

In order to defeat him, Twilight Sparkle had to give up her magic. It was this selfless sacrifice that gave Twilight and her friends access to the rainbow power locked in the Chest of Harmony.

Talking the Talk

Flim and Flam are fast-talking brothers who love to spin a line or two! These travelling salesponies are always making big claims they can't back up. They've got catchy jingles and big fancy machines with lots of bells and whistles, but they can't make apple cider as tasty as the Apple family's. And they certainly can't sell a tonic that will cure any ailment with one sip …

Don't Trust Trixie

Trixie is another pony who LOVES to talk, but often can't back up her words with actions! When the ponies first met her, Trixie boasted about being "the most powerful Unicorn in all of Equestria" and told them she had tamed an Ursa Major. Wow! But when faced with a real Ursa Major (or Minor as it turned out), it was soon revealed that she didn't know what to do.

Trixie Returns

When Trixie came back to Ponyville to get revenge on the ponies who had exposed her lies, she was much more powerful and even had glowing red eyes! She challenged Twilight to a magical duel – but soon saw the error of her ways and has become a much nicer pony.

DID YOU KNOW?

Trixie's father, Jackpot, was a famous stage magician. His most impressive trick was the Splashtastic Escape, performed with his friend Big Bucks. It's no surprise that Trixie loves magic shows too!

Foes and Their Powers
Best Bits!

"I am no friend. I am Lord Tirek, and I will take what should have been mine long ago."

Discord's betrayal allows Lord Tirek to capture the ponies ... all except Twilight Sparkle.

Queen Chrysalis and her hive of wicked little changelings.

Lord Tirek destroys the Golden Oak Library, Twilight's former home.

Wedding terror ... Shining Armor's beautiful bride Cadance is replaced by an evil imposter: Queen Chrysalis.

"Destruction was my talent and darkness was my cutie mark." – King Sombra

The ponies and Shining Armor flee looming King Sombra as an icy winter takes over Equestria.

"I am Nightmare Moon! I have but one royal duty now ... to destroy YOU!"

Rainbow magic unleashed ...The magic of friendship destroys Nightmare Moon for ever!

The monstrous Tantabus plagues everypony's dreams – until Princess Luna finally accepts herself and her dark past. Sweet dreams!

Foes and Their Powers
Best Bits!

Discord may have a villain's evil laugh ...

... but the ponies have come to know his playful side too!

Perfect Pets and Animal Companions

Awesome Animals

As well as dragons, centaurs, griffons, parasprites and other unusual creatures, Equestria is also home to some more familiar animals. Some VERY special creatures are BAFF (Best Animal Friends Forever) with the ponies.

Adorable Angel

Isn't Angel Bunny the cutest, cuddliest creature you've ever seen? But appearances can be deceptive, as beneath the innocent fluffy exterior lies a determined and very bossy bunny!

As animal companion to Fluttershy, Angel Bunny has a lot of competition from Fluttershy's other animal friends. Angel ensures he stays number one by supporting Fluttershy each and every day. He reminds Fluttershy of her appointments, persuades her to speak up and even takes on the role of coach when she is in training to conjure up a tornado!

Stare vs Salad

Although Angel Bunny can be very supportive, he is also a little spoilt at times. Once Angel refused to eat a delicious salad Fluttershy had made him, finally having a huge tantrum. Fluttershy ran out of patience and used the "Stare" to calm him down. Angel Bunny learnt his lesson and ate all the salad!

Working Winona

It's no surprise that hard-working Applejack has a hard-working pet. Loyal Winona is a true companion in every sense, accompanying Applejack on her work around Sweet Apple Acres and snuggling up with her in the evenings. Winona makes herself useful by rounding up stampeding cattle and she even dealt with some loose Pinkie Pies after Pinkie made clones of herself!

One of the Family

Winona loves the annual Apple Family reunion. She bounds up to each member of the family and gives them a huge lick. Not surprisingly this clever canine is also a huge fan of apples, and her favourite pudding is apple pie and ice cream.

DID YOU KNOW?

Gummy managed to deliver a letter from Pinkie Pie to Princess Twilight Sparkle without eating it. Well done, Gummy!

Give It Up For Gummy

It's hard to see how Gummy and Pinkie ended up together – Pinkie is bouncy and full of energy and Gummy doesn't really react to anything! But they do say opposites attract and Pinkie and Gummy are true pals.

Happy Families

Gummy lives with Pinkie Pie at Sugarcube Corner. He can only eat soft things as he doesn't have any teeth, but that doesn't stop him trying to chew almost anything in reach … including Pinkie Pie Pound Cake and Pumpkin Cake – Mr and Mrs Cake's young twins – like to ride on Gummy's back.

More Awesome Animals

Purrfect Pet?

Opalescence is a very classy cat, and adores her pony owner, Rarity. Opal considers herself something of an expert on fashion and if she doesn't like a design of Rarity's she has been known to hiss and spit! But if she does like an outfit she will rub her head against it and purr.

Fancy Favourite

Opalescence loves her stuffed mouse toy and it is NOT a good idea to take it away from her. When Rainbow Dash was trying to choose a pet, she challenged each of the contenders to find a way to steal Opal's mouse to prove how brave they were. Tank the Tortoise eventually managed the fearsome feat – though he did end up with a scratched shell!

Pet For a Princess

Owls are said to be wise and so it makes sense that Princess Twilight Sparkle has an owl companion. Owlowiscious is very helpful when Twilight is studying. With a happy hoot, he is always willing to get a book from a high shelf. He's also come to Spike's rescue on more than one occasion.

Tank the Tortoise

A tortoise might not seem like an obvious pet for a super-speedy pony, but Tank is loyal and kind, just like his special pony friend, Rainbow Dash. Plus, he has a special hover motor that he can strap to his shell, so he never gets left in Rainbow's dust.

Royal Companion

Princess Celestia has a pet phoenix named Philomena. After Philomena loses her feathers, she bursts into flames. Then, like all phoenixes, she is reborn with all-new feathers and a new lease on life.

Fluttershy's Confusion

When Fluttershy first met Philomena, the bird was coughing and losing her feathers. Fluttershy took her home to try to find a cure, but all her treatments made the bird worse. When Philomena burst into flames, Fluttershy burst into tears! Luckily Princess Celestia arrived and told her pet to stop misbehaving. Philomena emerged from the ashes, stronger than ever!

Pets Best Bits!

A dog is a pony's best friend ... Applejack loves her trusty sidekick Winona.

Bathtime buddies ... Spike wasn't sure about Twilight Sparkle's new assistant Owlowisicious ... but the two soon became friends!

Pleased as punch ... Gummy's first birthday party!

Animal chaos ... Spike tries his hand at pet-sitting!

Peewee is the baby phoenix Spike rescues – and later returns to his parents.

Bunny bother! Angel is not impressed when Fluttershy invites the Breezies to stay in their cottage.

The correct way to give Gummy a cupcake is to place it on his head ...

Super smooch! Pets can make even the toughest of ponies blush with affection!

Spike learns a lesson ... don't mess with Opal!

Pets Best Bits!

Stop that bunny! Angel Bunny gets on board the Friendship Express ... next stop: the Crystal Empire!

Owlowliscious feels decidedly off-colour after a day playing with the Cutie Mark Crusaders!

Watch out, Spike, there's a flying tortoise about!

Celebrations and Events

Special Seasons

Lots of Equestria's celebrations welcome in the seasons, or mark the time of year when an important job is completed or a special anniversary reached. Everypony loves to be part of the action ...

Sensational Summer Sun Celebration

The annual Summer Sun Celebration marks the anniversary of Princess Celestia imprisoning Nightmare Moon. The wicked mare tried to bring eternal night to Equestria but Celestia was able to overpower her and restore the sun to Equestria.

Changing Places

Each year a different city in Equestria hosts the Summer Sun Celebration. When it was Ponyville's turn, Twilight Sparkle was put in charge of organising everything. As we now know, Nightmare Moon escaped from the moon on the night of the celebrations – and the one thousandth anniversary of her imprisonment – and ponynapped Princess Celestia. Thanks to the Elements of Harmony, and the magical bond between Twilight and her five new friends, Nightmare Moon was banished once and for all, and the Summer Sun Celebration turned into a big party to celebrate Princess Luna's return to Equestria.

DID YOU KNOW?
After Princess Luna returned, the ponies had the idea for a Winter Moon Festival to celebrate. Now the royal sisters each have their own special day!

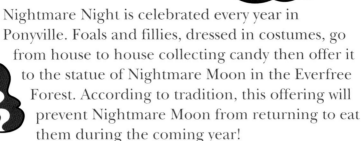

Fright Night

Nightmare Night is celebrated every year in Ponyville. Foals and fillies, dressed in costumes, go from house to house collecting candy then offer it to the statue of Nightmare Moon in the Everfree Forest. According to tradition, this offering will prevent Nightmare Moon from returning to eat them during the coming year!

Trick or Treat

On Nightmare Night, ponies enjoy a carnival, with music and games, including apple bobbing. Little Pipsqueak fell into the apple bobbing tub one year and was rescued by Princess Luna. The ponies were terrified, thinking that she was Nightmare Moon and wanted to gobble him up!

DID YOU KNOW?

Fluttershy hated Nightmare Night until her friends persuaded her to join in the fun. But she went too far, dressing up as scary Flutterbat and terrifying her pony pals!

Popular Princess

Arriving in Ponyville, Princess Luna couldn't understand why everypony was scared of her. She was so upset, she even threatened to cancel Nightmare Night. But Pinkie Pie showed her that the ponies ENJOYED being frightened on this special evening! Finally Luna was able to relax and enjoy having fun with her Ponyville friends.

"Together we shall change this dreadful celebration into a bright and glorious feast!" - Princess Luna

Happy History

Throughout the year, ponies young and old come together to celebrate the dramatic events of Equestria's past. Many festivities are shared by all, while some families, like the Apples and Pies, have their own special customs and traditions ...

Hearty Hearth's Warming

The winter festival of Hearth's Warming is celebrated throughout Equestria each year. It's a little bit like Christmas – the ponies decorate a tree, share gifts and spend time with their family and friends. But the celebration relates back to the earliest days of Equestria.

The History of Hearth's Warming

Many years ago, three ponies – each representing one of the three pony tribes – were forced to come together when a terrible blizzard destroyed their food and homes. The three formed a friendship and this created a magical heart-shaped "Fire of Friendship". The fire calmed the blizzard, which had been caused by windigos – winter spirits feeding off hatred.

In From the Cold

From that moment on, the tribes learned that the warmth of harmony and love can conquer the coldness of hatred and grief. After the leaders settled their differences, all ponies could finally live in harmony in their wonderful new land, Equestria.

Spring Cleaning

The Winter Wrap-Up is an annual spring-cleaning event where winter ends and spring is welcomed. The ponies wrap up winter to prepare for spring and this is always done without magic. The work includes waking up the animals from hibernation, helping the spring birds to build their nests and scoring the ice so that it melts easily. It's a very busy time.

Twilight's Helping Hooves

Twilight Sparkle was SUPER excited about her first Winter Wrap-Up – and was determined to do everything she could to help. But helping without the use of her magic was much harder than Twilight had anticipated. First she skated into a snow bank, then she got stung by a bee and was even sprayed by a smelly skunk. Yuck!

True Talents

Twilight was worried that without her magic she wasn't useful to anypony, but then she remembered her other great talent … organisation. With careful planning and top teamwork, the Winter Wrap-Up was finally done … and Twilight was given the new position of "All-Team Organiser" by Mayor Mare.

Partying in Ponyville

All the main towns and cities of Equestria have their own particular festivities, linked to important events or themes ...

The Ponyville Days Festival

This fun-filled festival commemorates the founding of Ponyville and it has a different theme each year. One year, the chosen theme was "Moving Forwards, Looking Back Together", and it was decided that the town's oldest building would be recognised with a plaque. The youngest member of Ponyville's first family would also be honoured with the official role of Festival Princess.

DID YOU KNOW?

Ponies often settle arguments with a game of "Horseshoe, Hoof, Rock". Horseshoe beats rock. Rock beats hoof. Hoof beats horseshoe!

Family Fallout

But this announcement caused big trouble. Applejack believed that Apple Bloom should be the Festival Princess as the Apple family had founded the town ... but Filthy Rich believed the honour should go to his daughter, Diamond Tiara, because the town was built around Stinkin' Rich's first store. Nopony could agree and everypony started squabbling!

Peace at Last

Luckily Twilight found a clever way to stop the fighting. She decided to honour Sweet Apple Acres as Ponyville's first residential building and the Carousel Boutique as the original location of Ponyville's first commercial building (as it was built on the site of Stinkin' Rich's first store). Finally, everypony was happy!

Family Appreciation Day

On Family Appreciation Day all the ponies of Ponyville take a little bit of time out of their daily routine to appreciate their nearest and dearest.

Grannies Are Great

One Family Appreciation Day, Granny Smith went into Apple Bloom's classroom to talk about their family history and how they were connected to the founding of Ponyville. At first, young Apple Bloom felt embarrassed by her elderly relative and her eccentric ways, but she soon realised how fascinating her story was and felt hugely proud – and appreciative – of her granny.

Daring Derby Day

For the Applewood Derby, young colts and fillies build racing carts out of Sweet Apple Acres' applewood with the assistance of an older pony. Then they race these carts on a racetrack with the older assistants as their passengers.

Cutie Mark Competitors

When the CMCs decided to enter the derby, they were so excited at the thought of working closely with their pony heroes, Rainbow Dash, Rarity and Applejack. But then the older ponies started taking over – even insisting on driving the carts in the final race! Eventually Rainbow Dash, Applejack and Rarity realised they had been thinking about themselves and not their younger friends. It was time to let the Cutie Mark Crusaders do things their way!

DID YOU KNOW?
The Applewood Derby takes the ponies all around Ponyville. There are usually plenty of pile-ups and the ponies always wear special helmets.

Canterlot Capers

No place loves a party more than the royal city of Canterlot, home to princesses Celestia and Luna ...

Canterlot Occasions

As you might expect from the royal city, Canterlot hosts some seriously chic events. Only the most fashionable and well-connected ponies grace these parties with their presence.

Canterlot Garden Party

The Canterlot Garden Party is one of the grandest high-society events of the year. There is always classical music playing, a delicious high tea is served, and everypony wears their very smartest outfit.

Rarity's Party Problem

When Rarity was invited to the garden party by Fancy Pants, a sophisticated Canterlot Unicorn, she accepted the invitation – even though it clashed with Twilight Sparkle's birthday party. But it turned out Twilight's party was held next door to the garden party and Rarity decided to go to both, without telling anypony ... Super sneaky!

Very Important Ponies

When Rarity's friends found out her secret, they decided to visit the garden party too – much to the horror of the snooty VIP ponies! But when Rarity saw the Canterlot elite turning their noses up at her Ponyville pals, she stood up for them, calling them "the most important ponies I know".

The Grand Galloping Gala

This lavish event is an annual royal ball held to celebrate the completion of Canterlot many, many moons ago. To attend this event, a pony must possess a golden ticket.

The Perfect Party ...

When Twilight and her friends were invited to the gala, each had their own ideas about how fabulous it would be. Pinkie Pie imagined a huge party filled with amazing snacks and party games. Rainbow Dash dreamt of performing at the gala with her heroes the Wonderbolts. Fluttershy was excited about meeting the exotic birds that lived in the palace gardens. Applejack thought that the gala would be the perfect place to sell her apple-based snacks, while Rarity dreamt of meeting her prince while wearing a gorgeous gown. Twilight Sparkle just wanted to spend more time with her beloved mentor, Princess Celestia!

DID YOU KNOW?

One year, Discord invited a troublesome friend to the Gala. The "Smooze" caused chaos, eating the guests' valuable possessions and covering the palace floor with slime!

... Or Not

But when the big night finally arrived, the ponies were very disappointed by the gala – it was actually really dull! The friends attempted to make it special in their own way, which turned the party into total chaos!

Royal Reprieve

Although the friends thought they had ruined their chances of ever being accepted into Canterlot society, Princess Celestia told them that she never enjoyed the gala ... and that the friends had made the occasion a lot more fun with their escapades. PHEW!

Joy and Sparkle

Festivals and traditions are very important to the ponies of the Crystal Empire, who sparkle like crystal when they are energised by joy and happiness ...

Sparkling Celebrations in the Crystal Empire

Once freed from the clutches of evil King Sombra, the Crystal Ponies had LOTS to celebrate! There are several important occasions in the crystal calendar which are enjoyed by every pony citizen, and which also play a key role in keeping the Empire safe.

The Crystal Faire

The faire is an annual event and one of the city's most important traditions. It is held every year to "renew the spirit of love and unity in the Empire". There are lots of fun and games to be had at the faire, including ring-tossing, crafts, candy corn, toffee apples, jousting and even a petting zoo!

The Heart of the Action

The Crystal Heart is at the centre of all celebrations held in the Crystal Empire. The heart is empowered by the happiness of the city's citizens – and so it is very important that the citizens experience joy and laughter.

Equestria Games

These prestigious sporting games are held annually in a different location in Equestria – and it is a great honour to be chosen to host the event. When the Crystal Empire was chosen as a contender for host city, the citizens were over the moon. They built a huge new stadium and the city was polished until it shone brighter than ever before.

Pony Preparations

Princess Cadance, ruler of the Crystal Empire, asked Twilight Sparkle and her friends to come to the city to meet the Games Inspector, whose job it is to decide if a city is fit to host the games. Rainbow Dash explained that the inspector, Ms Harshwhinny, would be judging everything very harshly – so all their preparations had to be just perfect and the inspector must be treated like a celebrity.

DID YOU KNOW?

When the Crystal Ponies discovered they were going to host the games, they were so happy that the Crystal Heart shot a rainbow-coloured beam of light into the sky!

Games Gone Wrong

When Twilight and her friends collected the wrong pony from the station, things were off to a very bad start. The real Games Inspector was given no special treatment at all. But in the end Ms Harshwhinny revealed that this had worked in the city's favour: because she had been treated in a normal way, she had experienced the best of the city. Her decision? That the Crystal Empire would host the next Equestria Games!

Heroes and High-Flyers

The Equestria Games is the most important event of the sporting calendar – but it doesn't always go smoothly! When a giant ice cloud formed over the Crystal Stadium, Spike used his amazing fire breath to save the Games!

Friendship and Fun

Friendship and Fun

Everypony knows that nothing is more important than friendship. But every friendship has highs and lows. Buckle up for some rollercoaster friendship moments!

Dragon love ... Twilight will always have a true friend in Spike.

Nopony understands the power of friendship better than Twilight's wise, kind mentor, Princess Celestia.

Power ponies save the day! When Spike's comic book comes magically to life, the friends spend a day as fierce and fantastic superheroes!

Hugging it out … Moon Dancer felt abandoned when Twilight Sparkle moved to Ponyville, but when Twilight returned to Canterlot they fixed their broken friendship.

The magic of friendship in action … The Elements of Harmony are activated!

"All right, ladies, let's show him what friendship can do!" Twilight and her friends worked together to defeat fiendish Discord.

True friendship is … taking a crash together. Pinkie Pie and Twilight hurtle down the snowy slopes!

More Friendship and Fun

Celebrating friendship the pony way!

When Rainbow Dash's daring aerial stunts land her in hospital, her friends are always there to cheer her up!

Friendship is ... giving your friend a tomato bath after they've been sprayed by a very stinky skunk!

In a "glass" of their own ... The friendship of Twilight and her friends is celebrated in a gorgeous stained glass window inside Canterlot Castle!

A soft landing ... Rarity and Spike were plummeting towards the ground before being caught in midair by their brave, quick-thinking friends.

Friendship is ... comforting each other when a scary villain looms!

Pampered pals ... The La-Ti-Da Spa is just the place to bond with your best (and most beautiful) buddies.

More Friendship and Fun

Friendship is like walking on rainbows ...

Party rivals Pinkie Pie and Cheese Sandwich become firm friends when they realise that the best events happen when you work together!

Buddies take a pony bow ... The six pony friends and Spike enjoy the audience applause after peforming their Hearth's Warming Eve pageant.

Love and Romance

Love and Romance

The course of true love doesn't always run smoothly, but when it does, it brings joy to everypony! Equestria has seen romances, crushes and the occasional disappointment in love. Here is a super-sweet taster!

Cranky Doodle Donkey isn't so cranky when he's reunited with his true love, and future wife, Matilda.

Romantic Rarity has a huge crush on Trenderhoof ...

... who only has eyes for Applejack. (She's less keen!)

Hearts and Hooves Day is the perfect moment to show a little love for your special somepony ...

... and the CMCs also take the chance to pair up their teacher, Miss Cheerilee, and handsome Big McIntosh! It's the perfect match ... for a while!

Spike's crush on Rarity is legendary ...

... he even framed the kiss that she gave him!

More Love and Romance

Rarity dreams of meeting her very own handsome prince one day ... Prince Blueblood would do nicely!

Princess Cadance and Prince Shining Armor's wedding was the most wondrous celebration of love that Equestria has ever seen.

Famillies are fantastic! Sisters Pinkie and Maud Pie could not be more different, but they love each other dearly!

True Talents

True Talents

Some talents are spectacular. Some are surprising. Every talent is special. The ponies have learned that their goals are worth striving for ... but only if they use their powers in the name of friendship!

Group hug! The ponies celebrate discovering their true talents ... which were the reasons their cutie marks appeared!

Purple power! Twilight activates her magic to save her friends and Equestria ... AGAIN!

Twilight saves the Crystal Empire ... and gets a tuneful song from her five best friends!

More True Talents

Nurturing by nature ... Fluttershy is skilled at caring for the very BIGGEST ...

... and very tiniest of creatures!

Fluttershy overcomes her nerves and discovers a talent for speed when she helps Rainbow Dash create a massive tornado ... that gives Equestria back its rain!

Two sides to every story ... Applejack proves that a pony can be strong ...

... AND sweet. AJ's tasty cakes are among the best in Ponyville!

Generous Rarity loves to make her friends feel great ... creating stylish designs especially for them.

With her amazing hairdressing skills, Rarity also knows how to make a princess feel, well ... just like a princess!

Secret skills ... Who knew our favourite baby dragon could play the piano!

Farewell, Equestria!

Hello there, friends,

Our journey through the magical land of Equestria has come to an end. Thank you for joining me and my best friends to explore all the wonderful places in our kingdom, and meet the amazing ponies and extraordinary creatures who live here – as well as a few super-scary foes! We've had so much fun sharing our favourite adventures with you, as well as telling you about the most important events in our history, and some of our hopes and dreams too. We hope you've enjoyed it as much as we have.

Please come and visit us again soon!

Love from,

Twilight Sparkle xx